DUEL THE DARKNESS FOR NIGHTMARE RULE

Books by Calvin Demmer

Short Story Collections
The Sea Was a Fair Master
Dark Celebrations
The Town That Feared Dusk
Her Heart Beats for Ancient Beasts
Through the Ravenous Night We Ride
Duel the Darkness for Nightmare Rule

DUEL THE DARKNESS FOR NIGHTMARE RULE

CALVIN DEMMER

TABLE OF CONTENTS

JELLY 7

MICKEY STRANGE 19

RED 31

DUEL THE DARKNESS FOR NIGHTMARE RULE..............47

KEEP THE BEAT 57

BLOOD IS RED 69

NEW SKULLS FOR THE OLD CEMETERY 81

COUNTDOWN TO EXTINCTION 97

THE SMALL HOURS BROADCAST.. 119

NESSIE LIVES 133

JELLY

Freelance reporter Reggie Wilson pulled up to the narrow, dilapidated home and compared the address with the note he had made on his phone.

I'm here.

Reggie killed the vehicle's engine. He was investigating a lead he had been given by a local snitch. A snitch he knew the cops would shake soon, so he'd paid the guy a few extra for the information and told him to hold off on spilling his guts until Reggie had checked the place out.

It's a cutthroat world. You gotta grab any advantage, man.

The house, however, looked dead. Reggie figured he would knock and pretend to be asking property questions all around the neighborhood, and if no one was here he would simply take a look around. Exhaling, he felt his pockets, making sure he had everything he might require.

As he climbed out of his vehicle, his cell phone rang. Frowning, he took the phone out of his pocket and looked at the number. He killed the call. It had been the sixth call from her in the last hour, the sixth call from his now fiancée, Christa, but she wasn't the problem. It was her mother that caused his stomach to turn. He placed the phone back in his pocket.

I have to get her damn mother out of my thoughts. Who cares what she thinks of me? I'm gonna marry her daughter, not her.

Being from a rough, poor upbringing, while her daughter had been born with pockets bursting with cash, was the main reason Reggie figured she didn't wholeheartedly approve of them. Christa had assured him that wasn't the reason her mother had reservations. "Great, so it's just me personally she doesn't like?" he had asked. Christa had simply smiled and said, "Give it time."

As he made his way to the house's front door, it hit him like a brick to the jaw. He cringed, realizing why Christa had been calling. Today he was meant to have lunch with her mother.

She's phoning me to remind me, like I'd forget.

He ignored the fact that he almost had. Cursing under his breath, he walked up the few weather-beaten steps to the house's front door. Reggie knocked.

Silence reigned. Reggie thought about knocking again, but instead he decided to take a stroll round the back. If someone caught him out, there were many excuses he could come up with for entering the property.

First, let's put the phone on silent.

* * *

The first thing Reggie noticed in the backyard—apart from the terrible state of the place—were the cardboard boxes.

Sheesh, you'd think this guy is moving.

He looked at some of the boxes piled along the right side of the yard's perimeter.

They all seem to be kitchen appliances and shit.

Either the person living here was opening one serious restaurant or bakery at home, or they had a place in town. Reggie grabbed his phone and took some photos of the boxes, while keeping one eye on the house's windows—he didn't need anyone taking photos of him.

Done, he proceeded to the back door, which had been warped and cracked from water damage. He reached out toward the door handle, pausing to make sure there were no curious neighbors.

All clear.

He turned the handle; the door opened.

Before crossing the threshold, Reggie considered his options. When he'd pressed Christa as to why her mother had an issue with him, she'd eventually caved. "She doesn't believe you're motivated or ambitious." Reggie had laughed, and they'd then experienced one of their first serious fights. He shook his head, bringing himself back to the moment.

Not motivated, huh?

Reggie pushed the door open farther, slowly, as he was wary of the creaking of old doors.

* * *

The first room was the kitchen. It was dark inside with the curtains drawn. Reggie's gaze shifted all over the white tiled room. There were barely any kitchen appliances in here—apart from the usual culprits like a small fridge, stove, and microwave. The contents of those boxes had found another home. Reggie inhaled the stale air. There was a faint smell that bugged him, triggering a warning within. He breathed in deep; his nostrils became irritated.

Reggie wondered if he should call out and announce himself, as he'd heard of a few cases where door-to-door salespeople had been shot, with residents later claiming they thought the salespeople were intruders. However, alerting anyone to his arrival would give away the element of surprise. If no one was here, he wanted to be in and out without anyone knowing any better and with any useful info safe in his possession. The snitch he'd gotten the info from wasn't always the most reliable, but there had been a noticeable drop in the volume of his voice when he'd told him about the strange man who lived here. Reggie decided on stealth and entered the next room.

He found the reason for the smell.

The horrific scene in the dining room caused an ominous heat to erupt in the core of Reggie's stomach, and before he realized what was happening, he had retched all over the white wall next to him. The stench of decay in the room seemed to get stronger. He shook his head while glancing at his breakfast gracing the wall—once toast and eggs, now mush.

Damn, rookie mistake.

He forced his gaze back to the dining room table.

The head of Missus Caroline Maloney—whom he recognized from a missing persons section in the paper—rested on a white plate. A circular hole greeted him from the top center of her head. Reggie took a closer look. He could see brains, but worse, there was a fork ready with another bite size of the gray matter. Reggie had found the home of the man the press had dubbed "the Brain-Eater." It wasn't the most original name, but sometimes simple was effective.

Reggie thought about all the missing person reports he had in a file on his PC back home.

How many of them found the same end?

For a moment the world around him seemed to dull, as if he were trapped in some bubble. His breathing became labored. He had stepped into something huge.

Pulling himself together, he took out his phone and carefully snapped a few photos. He needed to search the rest of the home before alerting the authorities.

Maybe there are other victims held captive or even better, maybe more gruesome discoveries to be found.

Reggie put his phone away and took out a can of pepper spray he had in his pocket. He had to be easy on the trigger; his impulse was to spray anything that moved or made a sound. Reggie had seen some bad shit on the job, but this morning was a thunderbolt to the senses.

* * *

The more he journeyed through the home, the more he felt he was alone. The plan was building in his mind. He would document everything he could, get into his vehicle, and alert the police. When they arrived he would assist them, which would also make him the first reporter on the scene. He would then document whatever he could while they investigated, and with that and the photos he had taken in the house, he would have a nice bundle to take to one of the papers. Reggie would make a killing, and the prospect of being offered a full-time job by one of them was electrifying.

How's that for motivation?

Noticing light shining from beneath a door in the far end of the passage, he froze. This wasn't part of the plan. Reggie stalked toward the door and gently pushed it open. He saw steps leading down.

A basement.

Reggie listened carefully. There was no sound.

Maybe this sicko just left the light on?

A rush of fear coursed through him. He wanted him to turn and leave immediately, but he kept on thinking back to what Christa had said regarding her mother's views on him.

I'll show her.

He readied the pepper spray before him and descended the stairs.

* * *

In the basement, even with the coast clear, Reggie rode out another shock. This time, however, the menu couldn't have been more different from that on the kitchen table. For all around him were boxes neatly packed on shelves. Inside the boxes were cups of Brainy Boys Jelly Treats.

Man, I love that stuff.

Reggie figured the killer must share his hankering for the sweets. The jelly treats had become so popular that it wouldn't be a surprise.

This sicko likes him some brains, and then jelly treats for dessert, but hell, he sure does have a lot of the product.

Reggie could hear a mechanical cycling sound, almost like an old washing machine. He looked to the far side of the room and noticed another door standing slightly ajar.

Doesn't surprise me this nutjob has a weird house.

Reggie approached from along the wall so that he could sneak a peek within. He could see all types of kitchen machinery in the room, blenders, mixers, freezers and so on. A frail old man stood at a counter, measuring some liquid in a jug.

Bingo.

Seeing no weapon near the old man, and having faith in his own strength, Reggie decided to act. Not only would he be the famous reporter who cracked the case, he would be the hero as well.

You gotta grab the advantage.

Reggie swung the door open and barged into the room. The man seemed oblivious to his entrance. Reggie noticed a kind of frying pan on a counter within reach of him. He grabbed it and turned back to face the man. He felt sufficiently armed, now holding the pan in one hand and the pepper spray in the other. Adrenaline pumped.

"Freeze," Reggie said. "Show me your hands."

The man was whistling under his breath, but the tune stopped. "Oh, well now, it seems you've finally found me," the man said. Still with his back to Reggie, he stretched his arms out. No weapons were visible, though one hand cradled a cup of jelly.

"What? What did you say? You talk funny," Reggie said, tightening his grip around the pan. He liked the feel of its weight. One good hit of this and the old man would be of no danger to him.

"I'm British. William John Wellington, the Third. And may I ask your name, good sir?"

"British? Man, you're a sicko, that's what you are. Don't think I don't know what you're up to."

"Well, we are all entitled to our opinions. May I have your name?"

"I am Reggie Wilson. I'm a reporter. I am placing you under citizen's arrest. I know you're responsible for all those people who have gone missing. I know what you do to them. I saw your sick show upstairs."

"Oh, but that is not all," William said. He turned around, indicating toward the jelly treat in his hand. "I make these, you know? Why else would I need all the appliances? Of course, I unfortunately can't hire any staff, as I assume they may disagree with some of the ingredients required."

Reggie watched the man take a bite of the treat. He looked old, slow, and weak. Reggie had full confidence this was his moment. The dark truth then dawned upon him. The appliances, the room with all the treats packed and ready to go. "You're one sick—"

"Come now. Are all the insults necessary?" The man smiled. "You see, Mister Wilson, the brains are the secret ingredient, a necessity. They help get the right consistency, the right texture. Don't tell me you have not savored the heavenly taste of one of these treats?"

Reggie pumped out his chest. "You're a nutjob. Your run is over. Product has been canceled."

The man's demeanor changed. His visage transformed to one of displeasure. He turned, placed the treat down, and reached for something on the counter. Reggie caught sight of the large kitchen knife the man was going for.

"Don't do it," Reggie said, trying to sound as commanding as possible, while within, his heart thundered. He knew trouble was coming. The idea of the man surrendering was out the door.

The man ignored Reggie and grabbed the knife. He turned back to face Reggie, his face flaring with anger. Reggie thought he even saw him snarl.

The man charged.

The pepper spray or the frying pan?

Reggie was surprised at the man's newfound agility and speed. He waited until the man was almost on him and dodged the knife, turning to face the man as he passed by. The pan was in his stronger hand, and as the man tried to turn back around, Reggie took a swing. The strike was as sweet as a home-run hit. The sound of contact echoed in the basement. Reggie watched the man's knees buckle, and then the man fell to the hard gray floor. For a split second Reggie felt bad for hitting an old man like that, but the feeling passed, and he gave the man a good kick in the ribs just to make sure he wasn't aiming a surprise attack.

Reggie found some tape to bind the man's hands and feet, and then added some around his mouth for good measure. He made his way to his car to alert the police as he had originally planned, but he stopped in the previous room of the basement that contained the boxes of jellies.

Minto Greeny Surprise.

He spotted the flavor he used to enjoy before he knew its dark truth. He couldn't resist and grabbed a small pack containing four cups of the jelly, and then continued to his car.

After alerting the police—who assured him they would be there right away—Reggie decided to call Christa. He felt a lot better than he had earlier.

"Hello?"

"Hey, babe. It's me. Looks like I will have time to see your mother for lunch."

"Oh, that's great. Everything okay at work?"

"Yeah, had a wonderful day, even broke a case. Just gotta sort out some final things here. I see good times ahead."

"Awesome, babe. You can tell me about it all tonight. I'll let my mother know you'll make lunch. Just remember what we spoke about and be nice."

"Of course, I even got her a little gift," Reggie said, tapping the jelly treats on his lap.

Christa's mother had been a thorn in his side for their entire relationship. Now it was time to get his revenge. Soon she would hear about his heroic feats, but knowing that she would get to enjoy the last run of the once-popular treats made his revenge even sweeter.

DUEL THE DARKNESS FOR NIGHTMARE RULE

MICKEY STRANGE

The sun sat high in the pellucid Floridian sky as a forgiving breeze cooled the surface of his skin. All around, the sounds of the neighborhood played out their regular parts. There was no indication this summer's day would be any different from those that had preceded it, and for most people, it would remain just another day. For Aidan Holland, however, he would always remember the day as the first time the strange man came around.

Aidan stood in his backyard, trying to get the neighbor's dog, Skip, to pay attention to his antics. When clapping his hands and throwing stones didn't work, he resorted to barking. He hoped his mother, Margaret, who was hanging sheets on the line, wouldn't hear him. The dog seemed oblivious to his new plan. Aidan barked louder.

"Stop teasing him," his mother said.

Aidan frowned and turned around, hoping she would see him pouting, but all he saw were white sheets dancing in the breeze.

"Mom?"

Aidan marched toward the wash line and moved the first sheet aside. The basket the bedding had been in stood alone. His mother must still be outside because she wouldn't leave the empty basket. A shadow passed behind one of the white sheets on the line ahead of him.

Aidan upped his pace and pushed past the sheet. There was no one there. He looked around. Nothing nearby could have created the shadow, which in his mind had appeared as the shape of a person. His heartbeat increased, and he rubbed his clammy hands on his pants while walking around the wash line. He yearned for the back door to appear in his view. When it did, he saw the once-open door was now closed.

Aidan stepped to the first sheet he had moved and lifted it. He stuck his head through and saw the basket was gone. Sighing, he realized he must have missed his mother, who he presumed was back in the house. He looked to the neighbor's dog and couldn't resist giving one last growl.

"Didn't your mother tell you not to do that?"

Aidan jolted and turned on the spot.

A gangly, pale man with a bald head, dressed in a bright red suit, was leaning against the brick wall separating the back and the front yard. The man fit perfectly in the triangular shadow that the roof and the wall created. The suit sparkled as though it had glitter all over it.

Aidan had never seen anything like it. "Who are you?"

"That's a good question, kid. A good question," the man said. He reached into his pocket and pulled out a white card. He flicked it toward Aidan.

The card fell before Aidan, but he remained still. He stared at the man's hand and saw light scars all over it. They were similar to the burn scars that Missus Partridge, a teacher at school, had suffered in a fire.

"Mom says I must not take things from strangers or talk to them."

The man smiled. "It's just a card. Not candy."

Aidan stepped toward the card and paused. He saw the same scars on the man's neck that were on his hand. The intrigue of the card managed to outweigh any trepidation, and he took another step, then picked up the card.

"Great stuff."

Aidan looked at the card. "It's got nothing on it."

"Yeah, kid, I know," the man said. He held his hands out. "Why don't you pick a name for me, and a number, then write it on the card. Anything you want."

Aidan, perplexed, looked toward the back door. An uneasy feeling had begun to push away the intrigue. He nodded, hoping to get the man going.

"Neat. Write me a nice name, something cool."

"All right, mister. I better get going now. My mom will be looking for me."

"You do that," the man said, turning toward the gate.

Aidan watched him leave. He was surprised when the man opened the gate to the front yard without making a sound. The gate always squeaked when anyone else opened or closed it.

With the man gone, Aidan placed the card in his pocket and retreated into the house. He was undecided as to whether to tell his mother about the strange encounter, because a part of him was concerned he would get in trouble for talking to someone he didn't know. When she handed him a soda and told him he could watch TV for a bit while she did some ironing, he had all but forgotten about the man.

It was only later that night when he remembered the card. Curiosity flooded his veins, and he crept out of bed in his pajamas, realizing where he needed to go: the bathroom. He searched the basket of dirty clothes; fortunately, his mother hadn't washed them yet. Aidan took the blank card out of the pants he had worn that day.

Back in his room, he put on his bedside lamp and considered what name and number to write. He looked around his room for inspiration and the first name came easy: Mickey. For the surname he went with Strange. Lastly, he needed a number. His eyes grew heavy, and he wrote the first number that popped into his head: 2009, his birth year.

* * *

The second time the strange man came around, Aidan was rolling a dirty baseball on the living room floor. His mother, twirling the ends of her curly blonde hair, sat on one of the cream-colored sofas holding a magazine. The magazine, however, wasn't the main attraction. Every few moments she would lift her gaze to the large window looking on the front yard.

Aidan noticed her eyes harden. Her top lip curled as she grew ever more transfixed on something in her view. Aidan, intrigued, got to his feet and walked toward the window. His mother pushed him, and he planted a leg back to keep himself from falling over. Stable, yet shocked by his mother's action, Aidan frowned at her.

"Go, go call your father," his mother whispered.

"Why? What is it?"

"Go now, Aidan."

Aidan sighed. He turned around and followed his mother's command, while she went back to staring out the window.

When he returned with his father, Lawrence, his mother told him to go wait in his bedroom. He didn't. Instead, he ducked behind one of the walls leading to the living room. He kept quiet, trying to calm his breathing as he waited to hear what was going on.

"There's a strange man outside," his mother said.

"Well, I don't see anyone."

"Lawrence, he was there. He put something in the mailbox."

"What did he look like?"

"Tall, slender, and pale—oh, bald headed—and he wore the most atrocious red suit I have ever laid my eyes on."

His father cleared his throat. "Margaret, what is so strange about that? He was probably just dropping off an advertisement or something."

"No. There was something not right about him. It's too warm for those clothes, and I, I felt a chill. He kept staring at the house. When I looked at him, well, I couldn't find his gaze. His eyes looked like white marbles."

"Rubbish. I am going to check the mail. I don't have time for your nonsense. We need to find you something to do. This sitting and watching the neighbors all day is unhealthy."

"Please, Lawrence. Be careful."

Aidan scooted behind a table in the passageway and watched his father exit the house. He counted down the seconds. It wasn't long until he heard the front door open again. He braced for the drama to unfold. His mother's fear had begun to creep into his veins.

No drama came.

His father was chuckling and made his way down the passageway. When he reached the living room, the chuckling had turned into a high-pitched laugh. The sound echoed throughout the home.

"What? Why are you laughing? Have you gone mad?" his mother asked.

"It was a real estate agent or salesman, left his card."

"Card?"

"Yup. He must want us to contact him if we're interested in selling or, heck, maybe he's selling some new gadget. Hear there are a lot of these types of guys uptown. There's a name and a number. The number doesn't look right, though. It's too short."

"Throw it away, Lawrence."

"No, no, just hang on. If the number works out, I want to hear what the man has to say."

"Please don't, Lawrence. He looked so odd."

"I want to hear who he is."

Aidan heard his mother bang her hand on a table.

"Well, if you choose to be stubborn, so be it," she said. "What's his damn name then?"

"Mickey Strange," his father replied. "Number is two-zero-zero-nine."

A frigid touch trickled down Aidan's spine.

* * *

The strange man was expected the last time Aidan saw him. His father had phoned the odd number, which surprisingly worked fine, and had set up a meeting with the man. Aidan was sitting watching television when the doorbell rang. His father walked past the room. When he returned the strange man was with him. The man acted as if he had never seen Aidan before, and Aidan did nothing to suggest otherwise.

His father grabbed the remote and switched the television off. "Aidan. Why don't you go to your room for a little bit? Mister Strange and I are going to have a talk."

Aidan didn't want to, but he could hear the commanding tone in his father's voice. He left the room, only to run into his mother, who was on her way to the living room.

Aidan decided to try his luck. "Mom, can I go play outside?"

His mother seemed rattled, but she glanced down at him. "Yes, yes. Just don't come in until our visitor is gone, okay?"

He nodded and turned on the spot.

Outside, he scanned the yard for a place to hide, a place where he would be able to eavesdrop on the conversation. He targeted a spot beneath one of the living room's windows. It wasn't without effort, as he had to squeeze behind a prickly bush to be close enough to hear. The first audible voice he heard was his mother's offering Mickey tea. Mickey declined and shot straight to the purpose of his visit.

"I am here to purchase this house from you. The previous owner has tabled an offer my superior deems to be more than fair."

Aidan heard the clinking sound of coins and then his father's voice.

"What's this? A bag of coins? You all right?"

"Yes, and they are gold coins," Mickey said. "The value of which is higher than the value of your home. Where I'm from, we don't deal with your kind of money."

There was a pause. Aidan sensed perspiration building on his forehead as he waited for someone to break the tomb-like silence. Even the neighborhood seemed to have been switched to mute.

"Wait, wait, wait," his father said. "Did you say the previous owner, Gwen—what was her last name now?"

"Watson."

"That's it."

"Correct, she is the one who made a deal with my superior. I'm placing the offer, however."

"It's impossible. She's dead," his father said. He lowered his voice. "She died in this very home, suicide I believe. It's why we got such a good deal."

"That may be, but the offer stands. The house is not something she wishes to remain for others since her...demise from this realm. She believes the memories within should be only for her and her family members that stayed here. She's not happy with new owners."

"Lunacy," his father said.

Another moment of silence. Aidan grew restless and was about to shift his awkward seating stance when he heard his father's unmistakable high-pitched laugh.

"You're some nut," his father said. "I am not selling. I got this place for a steal and that's that. You can tell whoever made such a strange bid along with their ridiculous tale that the answer is no."

"Are you sure you won't reconsider?"

"No. I will show you out."

"I think you are making the incorrect decision."

"Out with you. I've heard enough, and here, take your damn card with you," his father said. Aidan heard his father stand up. His favorite chair bumped against the wall.

"I know the way," Mickey said.

The front door handle turned. The door opened. Slowly, Mickey Strange stepped into the light of the day. Knowing he would likely never see the man again after the poor outcome of the conversation with his father, Aidan came out from behind the bush.

"Hey, mister, here's your card. The one I wrote on."

Mickey, oblivious to anything around him, kept walking on the path leading to the front gate. Aidan ran after him.

"Mister. I still have your card. I wrote a name and number like you said."

Mickey opened the gate and stepped outside the yard. Only then did he look back.

"You keep it," Mickey said.

Aidan, about to dart home, halted when he heard Mickey whistle at him.

"Listen, kid. Why don't you hang back a second?"

Aidan looked up at the man, curious about the suggestion. The man's face showed no sign of emotion. A peculiar rumbling echoed all around them. This was followed by a strange metal moaning sound, almost like the sound inside the deep-sea submarines Aidan heard when watching war films with his father. He turned around and saw a crack running across his backyard. The lightning-bolt-shaped fissure headed straight for his home. It disappeared beneath the house.

The house collapsed, whining and creaking as if it were crying in pain. There was barely any time to shout as Aidan, frozen, watched his home disappear into the earth. In the span of a few breaths, it had ceased to exist. Aidan was about to run to the hole that had appeared in the yard, when he felt Mickey's hand on his shoulder.

"Sorry you saw that, kid. This is for you. Best take it."

Aidan spun around. Mickey dropped the bag of gold coins into his hand.

"I gotta be off now. Take care, kid."

Aidan wanted to scream, but his voice failed him. Tears swelling in his eyes made his vision blurry. He saw the shape of Mickey walking away. Aidan threw the bag of coins into one of the bushes near the front gate and ran toward the hole.

Buried in the darkness, the house's remains were barely visible. Somewhere deep down there, in the dark, beneath the rubble, lay his parents. His heart panged within his chest as the thought that they were dead surfaced. He wanted to scream but barely had enough energy to breathe. The world spun around, faster and faster, as if he were on a carousel gone rogue. He took a few steps back and collapsed onto his rear.

The world was now a blurry haze and time seemed to lose all meaning. Aidan first heard and then felt his neighbors come to comfort him. The sounds of gasps and sobs were replaced by sirens. Aidan then heard police officers talking. The world around him sharpened. The officers spoke of caverns below the limestone, Florida's sinkholes, and a freak accident. They said no one could have survived the collapse. Aidan had heard enough. He stood, clenching his fists into tight balls.

Aidan told the officers about the strange man, how the man had visited, and what he'd heard the man and his parents talking about earlier.

"You're in shock, son," one of the officers said.

"No, no, no, he was real."

"What was his name?"

Aidan hit a blank wall in his mind. He racked his memories, searching for the name—a name he had given the man. He begged his mind to let him remember, but he found nothing. He had forgotten the strange man's name.

It hit him: the card.

He pulled it out of his pocket and handed it to the officer. "Here, here, it's also got his number on it."

The officer looked over the card. "Sorry, son, this card is blank."

Aidan reached for the card; the officer handed it back to him. He scanned it over, realizing what the officer said was true. The name and number had vanished.

The card was blank.

RED

Right foot. Left foot. Right foot. Left foot.

This had been the pattern I'd been performing for... the length of time escaped me. Ahead of me, a man performed the same hypnotised march. I couldn't say why I trailed him, nor could I recall when I'd begun to. It simply had to be. So, time had become immeasurable and my actions perplexing. Yet I continued: right foot, left foot.

Brain waves stayed near linear, as if I were on hold and awaited an operator to make the appropriate connection. If I tried to force it, it became a rookie attempt at moulding clay. I could see the outlines of something beginning to form, but before anything clear truly emerged, a new shapeless heap replaced it. This frustration caused me to grunt as I walked. Try as I might, I couldn't keep myself quiet.

A scratching sound warned me of activity on my left. The man in front of me heard it as well and stopped, turning to look at the front yard from where the sound had emanated. I followed his gaze. Whatever it was, it was small, but any sustenance would do when hungry. Like sniffing smoke in the air, I smelled it as clearly as if it had always been there. Meat and blood – the clean ingredients caused my vision to sharpen, even if the world became tinged with shades of red.

The man headed for the yard. That triggered something primitive within me. I grunted at him. He returned the favour, but it had no impact on me. All I wanted was to feed.

The creature, a mouse, scurried into view. It had been foraging between wilted plants and surveyed the area before bolting across the unkempt front lawn. The man stepped to a pile of chopped wood. The mouse was headed there. He reached out with his arms, appearing stiff and sluggish. The mouse moved fast; the man had no chance.

My arms had stretched out in front of me. My hands turned to claws. My body readied to pounce.

The man waited.

My insides burned in anticipation. I wanted the mouse so badly my mouth hung open, though no saliva dripped. My tongue's dryness rivalled a desert. An urge made me want to run and dive at the mouse, but another voice, from deeper inside, told me to wait and be ready.

The man's foot came down as the mouse tried to pass him. He caught the bottom part of its body. The little vermin's head exploded from the pressure.

The man had succeeded. When he kneeled to pick up his meal, a bomb detonated in my head. Crimson streaks shot like tendrils across my sight, devouring all other colours.

Now, a voice within screamed.

So overpowering were the reds in my vision that I had to determine where the man was by first distinguishing between the different shades of the colour. I launched at the mass I assumed he was, but he paid me no mind, his focus on the mouse.

When I tried to knock him over, he stood and grunted at me.

"Grrrrrr," I returned.

He roared a deep, guttural warning.

I sensed he was all bark and no bite. Yes, he had more tact than me on how to kill the mouse, but I was no critter.

He shoved me.

I pulled him closer and pushed him. He fell; his skin tore away from what was once muscle and bone. He moved to stand, but I kicked him continuously so that he couldn't. Ribs cracked. Bones snapped. Tufts of grey hair above his ears confirmed his weakness.

He turned over onto his back; his thin arms reached for me.

I could see the fading red in his eyes.

I snarled, kicking his arms.

Another *snap* came.

He didn't resist as I stood above him. I lifted my foot and brought it back down on his neck. There was a loud *crack*. One of his eyes popped out and dangled over his cheek.

I picked up the dead mouse and sniffed it. It was clean, unlike the man I'd killed. I stuffed it down. My jaw crackled as I crunched through little bones. The satisfaction was instantaneous.

When I'd consumed the creature, the red retreated. My instincts waned. I stood in a near trance for some time, looking around the grey world.

Eventually, I turned and stared at the road. It called me.

I left the front yard, stepping over the dead old man.

Once in the middle of the road, I could see its ever-expanding view. I lifted my right foot and placed it a step before me. I did the same with my left.

Right foot. Left foot.

* * *

I shuffled through fading light and darkness. By the time light came again, I'd passed many people, but all were dirty like the old man. I needed nourishment; the mouse had done nothing but make the hunger pangs worse, but no potential meals appeared. Relegated to survival mode, I waited for something to flick the switch to optimal performance.

Two elderly women appeared up ahead, sharing my hypnotised state. They were both dirty. I ignored them, but a weird sensation tickled my core. I couldn't explain it. I stopped, crooking my neck to the left. A street sign stood a few feet away. I couldn't read it, but it sent a spark of current through my head. I looked around, sniffing the air.

Something in this area intrigued me.

Instead of heading along the road, I took a left into a residential area.

The peculiar feelings only grew as I journeyed on. I grunted louder, trying to figure out what it all meant, but nothing came to mind.

One of the homes stood out against the rest.

I stopped.

Its wooden shutters stood open and it had broken windows, not unlike many of the other houses I'd passed. The place still felt unique, which ignited flames of curiosity.

I approached the home.

As I walked across the yard, another feeling, reminding me of static, crackled all over my body. I couldn't name this newfound emotion, but I had stopped grunting. I followed the stone path to the front door, which stood open.

Sticking my head into the home, I crooked my neck and sniffed the air. I didn't smell any clean meat, but something in this place called to me. I put my right foot over the bloodied mat in front of the doorway.

Sounds, like plates crashing to the floor, disturbed the silence. I followed the noise into a room with a tiled floor and light wooden cabinets. There was a broken sink on the far side, and a counter in the middle with junk piled on it. I couldn't recall the name of the room.

Two dirty ones, both male, smashed objects inside. There would be no sustenance to gain from them, but I couldn't simply leave. They shouldn't be here.

I managed to coax pale shades of red to enter my view. My shoulders hardened. I took a heavy step toward the intruders and grunted. They paid me no attention. I grabbed the nearest of them and pushed him back. When he tried to stop me, deep-hidden instinct kicked in, and I drove him to the closed back door, knowing if I pushed hard enough, he would go through it. It worked. The door broke free from its hinges. The backyard of the residence caught my eyes. The other one groaned as he ran past me to get outside.

The one I'd pushed had suffered a fracture to his left leg. The bone stuck out, reminding me of a broken branch. He couldn't stand, but I had no sympathy for him.

I grunted.

He whimpered, crawling away, trying to escape. His partner had already exited the backyard and was back in the street, where I knew he would perform the repetitive walk and head for a destination unknown. When I saw the one with the damaged leg dragging himself across the backyard, the red shimmer in my view receded. I turned around and entered the home. I wanted to find out why the place caused the strange waves within me. It was different to the red. It was more a switch begging for activation.

I moved throughout the bottom floor and came to a room with a couple of sofas, though one lay toppled over. They seemed to face a thin black box hanging upon the wall. I could recall clusters of packed info in my mind, but I couldn't unpack and arrange them in order. I grumbled in annoyance and clenched my fists.

A wooden shelf to my right had all types of things placed on it, but one of the items stood out. It was... rectangular.

I inspected the object, finding faces in it. They were clean ones and they... smiled, but they weren't really there. I held the fake object up. My clumsy hands failed me, and the object escaped my grip. I tried to juggle it. I caught one of its edges with my right hand, managing to get a view of the image before losing my hold.

A sensation of static electricity exploded in my brain.

The world jiggled as if made of jelly.

* * *

Memories flashed within my mind. Along with them, bits of knowledge surfaced. I'd dropped a framed photograph.

I focused, and slowly, like candles lit around a house during a power outage, rooms in my mind became illuminated. I knew the people in the photo. The man was me. I once had a name, a family, a wife, and a daughter.

The rooms in my mind dulled, and the flash of data that had come online after seeing the photograph receded. A thick haze spread throughout my mind, making thoughts cumbersome to hold on to and align. I wanted to fight, but slowly the other, overwhelming red force within me regained supremacy. I stood, staring at the broken frame on the floor. Shards of glass twinkled as light hit them. The strange feeling the house encouraged stayed, and I plodded to the window overlooking the front yard. I could hear noise, like patting on the ground. My senses heightened. Could this be a meal?

A female with long blonde hair ran on the road, past the window, carrying a type of bag. I didn't have to smell her to know she was clean. It showed by the way she moved. I wanted to scream and smash through the window, but I remembered the patience of the old man and the mouse.

The woman looked my way, briefly, but she couldn't see me. The red assured me so. I, however, had seen her clearly. Her face stained my view. The energy the red disapproved of coursed through me again. My body threatened to collapse, and my mind wanted to black out once more, but I battled the red. I had to know where she was going.

A few houses down, she turned into a yard. A house that had looked dead came alive. Another clean one, a man, opened the front door. He held a long object – a weapon – in his hands. She brushed past him to get into the home; he looked around the neighbourhood before entering and closing the door behind him. The home morphed back into one of the many lifeless houses lining the street.

My first plan was to rush over there and smash through the door. I desired meat and blood. Hunger wanted me to go to war, but I tried to whisper reason to myself. I had to force my mind to search for a smarter way. I had to get in.

I couldn't fail.

It took a long time. The light left. The dark came. Internal processes moved at glacial pace. I had to constantly fight off urges to bolt to the home keeping the clean ones. A plan came. It was simple, but I sensed it could be effective.

The red agreed.

* * *

Under the cloak of night, I left my home. It proved harder to leave than I'd imagined, but I had another fixation, another hunger. I exited from the rear, not wanting any of the clean ones to see me. My goal was to enter the backyard of the house inside which *they* hid. This task wasn't easy and took a great deal of time, as I had to look out and sniff the air for any slight variations. I was fearful I would lose my position and fall under the spell of the road again. I had to keep to the shadows as much as possible, which was not easy considering my limited mobility, but I managed.

The gate to the backyard was my first obstacle. It didn't budge when I pushed it, and a chain had been locked around it, but farther along, I sighted a broken spot in the fence. I made my way there, careful to avoid the light.

A sharp type of wire had been secured to the bottom of the broken fence, likely a hack-job at attempting to fix it. I pulled on the wire, stopping when one of my fingers dangled from my hand. I hadn't felt the pain, and no blood came.

I ripped off the finger and threw it behind me. With effort, I removed the wire. The female with the long blonde hair had intrigued me. I would devour the male first, however. I assured the red within of this. It had crept back to the surface as I neared the house, and I could not usher it away; I needed it. It brought its ability to see and do things I normally couldn't.

In the backyard, there weren't many places to hide. I also had to push myself to step at a faster pace. It wasn't easy. My body commanded that I adhere to its need for energy preservation.

I found a spot a few feet from the back door, against the same wall, where I could hide in shadow. I looked around, and the red agreed no windows threatened me. This was a good spot.

My simple plan had begun. I pushed my forehead against the wall, unable to determine if the surface was warm or cold. I would wait until someone opened the door, and then I would strike. The yearning for clean flesh never truly left, but I could keep it under control. I doubted whether I could keep it at bay forever.

* * *

Light came, and with it my hiding place retreated. I inched closer to the door, wanting an advantage to pounce, while lowering myself, which wasn't an easy task with heavy and awkward legs. I found a spot, hidden behind a plant a good jump from the door. The tingling energy flowed within, not as potent as I'd experienced at the other home, but strong enough to help keep me alert. The red had gone back to hiding, but it could reappear within the blink of an eye.

A noise I didn't understand came. It was from a small one of them, but it wasn't grunting. It was higher in tone and nonthreatening. I heard more noise, and I grasped these were voices. The clean ones communicated. My body threatened to leap up, and I had to force myself against the wall, pushing myself down. Now was not the time. The red had briefly appeared, assuring me the people within were oblivious to my presence. Their relaxed voices confirmed this. There was no scent of fear.

I don't know how much time passed, but their voices disappeared. I had to fight through another round of wanting to get up and attack the door. I suffered a few of these waves. The people didn't leave the house either; I assumed they had the sustenance they required within, but nothing lasts forever, and they would have to leave eventually.

The red assured me if they left from the front, I would hear them. That wouldn't be ideal, but I could still come undetected from the side of the house. This spot still seemed best. The red agreed. The woman may have only used the front door the previous day as a last resort, which would explain why the man had come out with the hardened actions of one concerned, but prepared for action. Yes, this was the right place to be. Other, deeper thoughts dared to awaken, but the red retreated, before anything substantial could form.

I went back to my standby mode, to wait it out, when footsteps sounded from within the home. My vision had traces of pink, and I knew the red didn't want to return so soon after I had tried profounder introspection, but no alternative ideas emerged; the time had come.

My hands curled. My shoulders tensed. The footsteps became louder, pounding within my head. Aromas teased my sense of smell. I could almost taste them. They were clean, so clean. I couldn't tell how many of them approached, but there were more than two. Streaks of red squirted before my view.

The footsteps neared.

The door handle turned.

The man exited the house, cautious and on edge. He held the weapon and scanned the backyard. It took a great deal of effort not to throw myself at him.

He signalled back at the house.

The woman peeked out, but the man put up his hand.

I feared he'd sensed me, and I couldn't contain myself.

I grunted when launching at him, knocking over the plant behind which I'd been hiding, as well as empty flowerpots in my way. The man tried to point his weapon at me, but I pushed him back, sending him crashing to the floor.

The woman screamed and retreated. I rushed after her into the house, putting the man to the back of my mind. My vision flooded with shades of red. A range of smells overwhelmed, noises boomed, but all I wanted was to get to her. She ran into a large room, similar to the one in the other house where I'd passed out. The sounds and voices cleared.

"Someone help me!" she screamed, scurrying behind one of the sofas.

I grumbled in return.

She turned around, and as though I'd taken a punch to the gut, the world around me wobbled. There was a uniqueness to her.

She looked at me, having ceased screaming. "Andrew?"

I'd ended my pursuit and stood like a statue in the centre of the room. The name sent a bolt of electricity across my chest. It hit me. Her name was Sarah.

I tried to say her name. "Grrarrghha."

I walked to her. My arms reached out. The haze in my mind cleared; she was my wife. I wanted to comfort her, but I halted a few steps before her when I perceived my appearance.

Something struck the back of my right knee. I felt no pain but knew by the instant view of the ceiling my leg had given way. I landed on my back and moaned in frustration. Who dared to stop me when I was so close to comforting my wife? A face hovered above me, and I remembered I had a daughter. Her name was Rachel.

She stood over me, holding a baseball bat. "Dad, is that you?"

I didn't know how to communicate. Inside, the red raged. Its true intentions had united with near-surface primal instincts. It wanted to hunt, kill, and devour. I had to keep the red from tearing everything to shreds, while still extracting some of the power that came with it. Fortunately, the other current resurfaced. It gave me a fighting chance. This strange electric feeling had pulled me along and guided me as much as it could. The red couldn't eat and destroy it. It fought deep within me, when I no longer could. The new player inside had become stronger as I had gotten closer to my family.

"That's not your father," the man from the backyard said. "He's a zombie. He has already turned."

I searched through memories, trying to figure out who he was. He made his way to my wife and daughter, telling them to shush and breathe and that he had it all under control. He'd replaced the weapon from outside with another. I knew this one: a spade. He had changed weapons to make less noise when he tried to kill me. I wouldn't let him succeed, not when my family was so close.

I tried to get up, but the damage to my leg had been severe. The man noticed my attempts and stood above me, placing his foot on my chest. He raised the spade, aiming the sharp digging section for my neck.

My daughter cried out.

"He's not your father, damn it," the man said. "We're putting him out of his misery."

My wife held my daughter close, turning her head so she wouldn't see what happened next. I grabbed the man's leg but couldn't get enough force to budge it. I tried screaming, but all that came out were more grunts. I understood how I looked and knew it didn't help me, so I stopped.

I fought the red. My vision cleared.

"Look, he's not fighting back," my wife said.

"It's a tactic," the man said. "He's a smart one, a dangerous one. He's not your husband."

With every power in my being, I tried to speak the words "I am," but they wouldn't come. Gargling sounds left my mouth instead. I tried to say my name, "Andrew," while looking at my wife.

"He's trying to speak," she said.

"Bullshit," the man said. "He's trying to bite."

The man looked at me. His face hardened.

I knew him. He was our neighbour, Tim. He was the asshole who used to make unwelcome advances on my wife. The same Tim who, when drunk, had made her so uncomfortable at a neighbour's BBQ with his incessant flirting, I'd had to step in. The virus must have given him his chance. My wife and my daughter probably didn't have anywhere else to go but to the son of a bitch, Tim…

Tim, the son of a bitch, brought down the spade.

I tried to shout as the spade cut into my neck, but once more, all that came out was grunting.

The red vacated my body.

It no longer had a host.

The other energy, love, held me, as a darkness ate the world.

DUEL THE DARKNESS FOR NIGHTMARE RULE

A ghostly zephyr caressed the nape of Lewis' neck as he surveyed the discovery before him. He glanced at the circular window to his right. It was shut and covered in dust. Maybe he had only imagined the breeze? Moments ago, he had been searching the attic for a box containing kitchen utensils when he'd taken a wrong step. The creaky wooden floor had given way, but he hadn't fallen through to the room below. He had, however, fallen backward and bumped his head on an old wooden chest. After pushing through the vertigo when he stood, he felt his head for blood—there was none. A small, sensitive bump pained when under pressure from his fingers.

Inspecting the floor, he found that he had only broken the surface planks, revealing a dark object underneath the wrecked boards. "What the...?" he muttered as he knelt. He wasted no time in removing further pieces of the floor to expose as much of the peculiar object as possible. More dusty items presented themselves. They all appeared to be types of armor. A knight's armor? Definitely. Was it real or a replica? It looked as if it had endured much usage—maybe even seen battles? Perhaps buying an old home had its little rewards after all.

"Please be real," he said.

The armor wasn't without a host. A skull lay at the top of the archaic ensemble. Would he have to report the remains? Surely, he would be required to. Why did that have to be there? A long object shimmered beneath the armor, drowning any negative thoughts rising to the surface of his mind.

His hands shook as he retrieved the item. "Holy shit, a sword."

Lewis admired the long blade, the thin guard, and the black grip with its faded pattern. The sword was a beautiful work of art—intended for battle. He raised the weapon above his head, imagining himself as a knight in combat. A pain shot behind his eyes as a swell of nausea rose from his gut. He wobbled forward, then back. The world shook and shattered before him, as if some malignant force had ripped all the particles apart. In their place a black cloud swirled and swallowed his view. As it cleared, almost as fast as it had enveloped him, he saw luscious green hills all around him. Aromas of earth and fire invaded his sense of smell. The *clangs* of steel on steel, the *thuds* of steel on wood, and the shouts and shrieks of men at war called his attention to his right.

A bloody battle raged between two armies in the distance—many of the soldiers wore knights' armor.

He dropped his gaze; he still held the sword.

"Sir Lewis, are you injured?"

"What?"

A knight walked toward him. "You have wandered away from the battle. That is unlike a knight of your caliber. I thought you may be wounded."

"Um...I..."

The sky above the battlefield darkened, as if storm clouds had assembled with haste and fury. A bitter taste overwhelmed Lewis' mouth. The knight had disappeared. The battle had vanished. The darkness spread all around him, until it engulfed all his being once more.

"Lewis, are you okay? What happened?"

"What?"

"You were unconscious."

Above him stood his wife, Abigail. He was about to say her name when he realized he never called her by her full name. Her auburn hair fell over her pale shoulders as she leaned forward.

"Are you okay?" she asked.

"I'm fine, Abi. I think I found something."

She aided him up, and he rested on one knee. The sword and the armor were gone. All that remained was the hole in the floor. "So odd," he muttered.

Abi said, "I found the box of kitchen stuff in the spare bedroom. I'm sorry about sending you up here for nothing."

Lewis wanted to tell her about the sword and armor. He wanted to tell her about the battle he had witnessed. Instead he kept quiet, knowing that Abi wasn't into the mysterious or weird. If he had no proof, it would be a trivial exercise.

"Let me help you back down to the living room. Then I can give you a proper check over."

"No. I want to sit here for a second."

* * *

It was rare in England for the heat to rise into the temperatures it did later that week, particularly in the area where Lewis and Abi lived. Abi had opened all the windows, inviting a breeze to cool them.

"That's not the painting I wanted," Abi said, entering the living room.

"What do you mean?" Lewis turned to the painting he had hung. A large castle draped in shadows sat atop a hill. The castle overlooked a flowerless meadow sparsely populated by ashen-colored shrubs. Darkening clouds gathered in the sky to the castle's right. "It's one of yours."

"No." Abi shook her head. "Yesterday you told me you found it in the attic. I told you that you should've left it there."

Lewis didn't know what Abi was talking about, but he didn't want to enter into a fight with her. "You don't think it looks nice?"

"It's not our style. Didn't you see the painting of the seaside village I placed on the bed? That's the one I wanted for here."

The sound of a vase shattering on the dining room's tiled floor drew Lewis' attention to the doorway on his left. A fox, with reddish fur, triangular ears, and a pointed black snout, trotted into the living room. The fox turned to face Abi. It snarled, revealing white foam around its mouth. There was something off about its eyes, as if they flickered between red and yellow.

"Get back," Lewis ordered Abi.

"Why?"

"There's something wrong with it."

Before Lewis could move, activity to his right alerted him. At first all he saw was black smoke, but it dissipated as heavy *thud*s echoed from the steps of whoever had marched into the living room. A person, dressed from head to toe in armor, now stood between Abi and the fox. The stench of brimstone hung in the air.

"Who...who are you?" Lewis asked.

The person didn't answer. Instead they raised their arms, revealing a sword. The armor and sword appeared eerily similar to that which he had seen in the attic. Could it be?

The person moved for the fox.

They swung their sword.

So mighty was the blow that crimson blood splattered all over the living room. The fox, killed by the one strike, collapsed on the floor. The intruder, seemingly satisfied, turned around and began strutting out of the room.

Lewis stepped in front of them. "Hey, who the hell are you?"

The person pushed Lewis.

Lewis fell backward, grasping at the empty air and astonished by the strength of the intruder. Unable to prevent his fall, he braced for impact and managed to get his hands to the ground first, protecting his lower spine, but was forlorn in his attempt to prevent the back of his head from banging against a small table. Blackness invaded his peripheral view, and a rocking lightheadedness preceded the rest of his sight fading to black.

When his vision returned, hazy at first, Abi stood over him. "Lewis, why did you do that? Are you okay?"

He caught sight of the castle painting on the wall, to Abi's right. It was covered in specks and streaks of blood. The new red additions to the piece only seemed to highlight the castle even more.

"I'm fine."

* * *

The next weekend, tears streaked down Abi's face upon her arrival home. In anger, Lewis demanded to know the reason for them. He already knew she had been to her father—this wasn't the first time she'd returned in such a state after visiting him. When she went to the bedroom to sob on the bed, he ceased his investigation. Instead of taking a seat next to her until she was ready to talk—which was normal protocol for when she was distressed—Lewis jumped into his vehicle and drove until he came to a small face-brick home. The house looked identical to the others around him, but inside this one dwelled his foe.

He banged on the house's white front door.

Abi's father stepped out, causing Lewis to retreat a few steps. "What the hell do you want? You're bugging me when I want to be relaxing."

"I'm here because of Abi. You keep treating her like shit. I've had enough of it."

"Oh, now you've all of a sudden grown some balls." Abi's father placed his hands on his hips. He surveyed the neighborhood. "How about you fuck off right now or I knock some real sense into you?"

The stench of alcohol rode the man's breath.

Lewis asked, "What did you do this time?"

"I told her I didn't have the old photos of her mother. I don't keep shit like that around. I tossed all the crap when I moved. Now, piss off!"

Lewis grabbed Abi's father's arm instinctively. The old man's eyes widened and then a snarl formed on his face. He pulled free of the grip and pushed Lewis with enough force that Lewis would've landed on his rear were it not for his younger reflexes.

A figure in Lewis' peripheral vision, on his right, drew his attention. He observed the newcomer. The person dressed in the knight's armor had found him, except they took no notice of Lewis and marched toward Abi's father. They plunged their sword into Abi's father's chest before he could dodge or retreat. Blood exited the wound, splattering over the stone path leading to the house's front door. The person in the armor turned and walked away as if they had been a postal worker delivering the mail.

Lewis moved forward, unsure what to do. Should he call for an ambulance? Should he cover the wound? Abi's father had toppled forward and was gurgling and holding his chest to no avail—the blood kept coming.

"Shit." Lewis reached for his cell phone while glancing to see where the assailant was: the person was gone from view. How was that possible? No one could move so fast, especially not in armor. He dialed the ambulance and was about to speak when Abi's father yanked his left leg. This time, his reflexes failed him, and he fell backward.

He braced for the impact.

* * *

As Lewis awoke, his surroundings caught him off guard. He lay in a barren, white-walled room. Except for the hard mattress and bed, there were no other objects in the area. He sat up and stared at the door across the room. How long had he been out for? How had he come to be here? A face appeared behind the large panel of glass in the upper middle of the door.

"Abi, is that you?"

"Lewis...you're awake..." Abi's voice sounded tinny. Brief bursts of white noise followed her pauses.

Lewis looked up, locating a small white speaker above the door. He got to his feet and made his way toward her. "Abi, what the hell is this? Where am I? How long have I been in here?"

"It's been a couple weeks. It's for your own good," Abi said from behind the glass.

"What are you on about?"

"The knight you keep talking about. The things you keep doing. You were arrested after your last incident and eventually brought here."

"Incident? You've seen the knight. Remember the fox? It was sick. The knight killed it in front of both of us."

"No, Lewis. There was no knight who killed the fox that day. It was you. You hit it with a cricket bat. I tried to tell you it was fine and more scared of us and that it would leave. But...you were already not yourself. I should've done something sooner. I—"

"What about the knight attacking your father?"

"No, Lewis. That was you again. You stabbed him with a knife. One of the neighbors saw the entire altercation. He barely survived. You're not well."

"I am fine... I am."

"Can't you just snap out of it? You were never the same after that day you fell in the attic. We should've done tests or something. I should've... Why can't you stop this knight bullshit? Why can't you beat it?"

Duel the knight? Duel the darkness? That was madness. Perhaps it was Abi who wasn't thinking correctly. Maybe the knight's presence had affected her even more than him. "Abi, when last did you see the knight?"

"I've never seen a knight. Are we going to do this again?"

"Abi, please just—"

"Snap out of it! Now!"

Abi's raised voice hit hard, breaking through barriers in his mind. A bitter taste surfaced in his mouth, a burnt smell teased in the atmosphere, and then a dull pain throbbed in his forehead. Images of a bloody battle, of a castle atop a hill, of his sword, of his armor, swirled within his mind.

"Did you hear me?" Abi asked. "Snap out of this bullshit."

Lewis nodded.

He glanced at the stone walls that imprisoned him. Then he beheld the jail's bars keeping him from his love. Years of hard battles seemed nothing in comparison to his current predicament. He missed his armor. He missed his sword. A knight was lost without such things.

He knelt.

"I'm sorry, Lady Abigail. I've failed you. I accept my fate."

KEEP THE BEAT

Dusk would fall, and the sounds of the djembe drums, which ranged from thuds to slaps, would commence. First, it was only one or two drums in the distance, but within minutes, Aminata heard the beat all around her. It was a simple pattern, which would not cease until night had blanketed the world.

As she watched some of the villagers of her tribe prepare fires to cook, it dawned on her she had never questioned why the drums were brought out. Tonight was different. The question of why had stuck. She inhaled wood-scented smoke from the fires. Why did people go separate directions into the jungle to sit alone and play? Were the people that left merely providing amplified entertainment for the rest of the village while they cooked? There was no singing along with the beat as was usual when instruments were played—though she did hear a few people mumble along. As soon as it was dark, the drums stopped, the people returned, and then everyone ate.

Every night.

"You're not wrong to question it," Idrissa said, taking a seat alongside Aminata in front of one of the fires. "In fact, it's a good sign. It shows you're ready."

"Ready for what?" Aminata asked.

She had waited for Idrissa, one of the male elders she got along with best, after deciding to investigate the peculiar ritual. He was tall and muscly, which were common features among the men in the community. The drums had already started up their beat as the two sat in the gray world.

"You're ready to know more." Idrissa reached for a stick and held it over the fire. Smoke rose from the end of the stick. "Maybe, you are even ready to participate."

"I'm ready." Aminata didn't feel the desire to hit on a drum, but if it led her to uncovering why they were played, she was prepared to feign interest.

"Hmm. Perhaps you are ready."

"I am, Elder Idrissa."

Idrissa looked to the heavens. "Do you believe in ghosts?"

Aminata frowned.

"Have you ever wondered why we take the ill or severely wounded beyond the mountains?"

"You take them to the land of peace, to die. Like you did with my parents when they were ill and could not be healed."

"Yes. That was a sad day. You were brave. But there is more to it. The mountains surrounding us are special. You see, if a person dies in the valley, their spirit can't move on to the next realm. They remain stuck here. We believe they live in caves in the mountains, and they're only able to roam the land at dusk."

Aminata smiled. She didn't know how to respond to the ridiculous tale. Why could an elder never be direct? She would have to go through an entire procession of some age-old myth before she'd ask one of the younger adults, who'd then give her a straight answer. She bit her lower lip, regretting not going to one of the younger adults first.

"But," Idrissa said, making a fist. "Not all the spirits in the valley are friendly. A few warriors from tribes that once ruled these lands, or warriors who attacked our very tribe, remain."

Idrissa picked up a djembe drum near him. Softly, he tapped the beat Aminata knew well. It was the same beat she heard every evening at dusk.

Every evening.

Idrissa stopped. "That beat. These drums. They protect us during dusk. Our village has been performing the ritual ever since we first moved to the valley."

Intrigue lit a flame in Aminata's mind. She didn't believe the tale. Evil ghosts roaming the land at dusk were a step too far, but she couldn't resist asking a question.

"What happens if the beat isn't played?"

"Bad things." Idrissa placed the drum on the ground. He seemed reluctant to release his grip, and his fingers trailed over the drum's animal skin. "You see, Aminata, not only must the djembe drums be played every night correctly, but there can be no area in our defense where there is silence. The wrong type of ghosts will find that spot, and…"

"Aminata. Aren't you going to eat tonight?"

Aminata turned.

Didi, one of the elder women, stood with her hands on her hips.

"Yes," Aminata said.

"Come then."

"Don't worry." Idrissa patted her shoulder. "Tomorrow, I will have a surprise for you. I will discuss with the other elders first, but I believe you are indeed ready for the next step."

Aminata nodded.

She followed Didi. Her stomach growled as her mind tingled with many thoughts awakened by the old myth. She hadn't received the truth, but she believed she'd obtain the real reason from one of the young adults. What she had received was a peculiar story, and now, she wanted to know why there was such a strange tale in the first place.

Was it covering up something else?

* * *

Aminata was assigned to Marie the following night. This suited her, as Marie had always been friendly, patient, and knowledgeable about the tribe's history and ways. It was the perfect set of circumstances for her to uncover the truth. A night's rest had not changed her mind on Idrissa's myth. Sure, it sounded fantastical and alluring, but it wasn't a practical reason. Aminata wanted more. She would accept any logical reason, even if just ceremonial, but not ghosts.

"Take a seat," Marie said.

Aminata did as instructed. The two of them had entered the jungle, leaving the tribe behind. They hadn't journeyed too far, but there was enough distance between them and the village that Aminata wondered how they would hear the other drums. The jungle also had its own music at night, from frogs croaking to insects buzzing.

"Are you comfortable?" Marie asked.

Aminata nodded.

"You must always be sure you are comfortable. You may not get the chance to move again, especially once the beat has begun."

"I'm fine," Aminata said, unable to resist shifting, carefully, hoping not to attract Marie's attention. If she was honest, she did feel a slight strain in her leg. The ground was hard. Soon, her rear would be numb.

"This is my spot," Marie said. "I know it well. You see that tree over there?"

Aminata followed Marie's gaze. There were markings carved on its trunk she didn't recognize.

"I know exactly how to get here. I know my spot. You will also have your spot. You must know it better than you know the ceiling of your hut."

Marie handed Aminata a djembe drum, and then sat with her own drum. "Soon, the beat will begin. Do not play along until you are ready. Start soft. Watch what I do and try to focus only on your drum. If you see anything in the jungle ahead of you, ignore it. Do you understand?"

"Yes," Aminata said.

"Good."

The beat came.

It began soft, mostly slaps, but as the beat intensified, it became an attack of heavy thuds, almost like a battle song.

Marie didn't hesitate. She tapped and slapped the drum with an educated ease. At one point, she even closed her eyes as if in a trance. Aminata yearned for the real reasoning behind the ritual while she looked at the jungle ahead of her, awaiting the okay to play along.

She saw no ghosts.

It seemed a peaceful night.

"Are you ready?" Marie asked.

Aminata turned to her and nodded.

"Start soft and slow. Let's see how much you know."

Aminata played along with Marie, getting louder and louder. There was something captivating about the beat once she got into a tight rhythm. The song bordered on the hypnotic, but still, she couldn't fathom it was anything more than a simple practice the tribe had yet to grow out of.

A shape moved between two trees in front of her.

Aminata stopped.

"Why did you stop?" Marie asked, not missing a beat.

"I saw something."

"I told you not to look into the jungle. The ghosts walk all around the protective field the beat creates, looking for weak spots."

"It looked like a boy."

"No." Marie slapped the drum harder. "It was a ghost. Now, continue playing and do not stop."

Aminata picked up the beat again. She couldn't cease scanning the jungle, searching, hoping, to see the boy again.

"The ghosts are all evil," Marie said. "I know some of them look friendly, but they're not. If I were to die in the valley, I'd come back as one of them and try to kill you."

Aminata didn't doubt Marie's attempt to frighten her for stopping the beat, but her curiosity had been piqued. "Why?"

"Ghosts have to move on. If they don't, they hate the living and wish to do them harm."

It was nonsense, but Aminata figured the tale scared the gullible. She thought of the boy, who had looked her age but was built strong with wide shoulders. His eyes were dark, unwavering. The boy had only briefly looked in her direction, but it was enough to create the feeling of butterflies in her core.

He wasn't a ghost. He was a real boy.

And not from her tribe.

Aminata had forgotten all about the ritual and how it supposedly came to be. All she could think of was the boy.

* * *

"This will become your spot." Idrissa waved his hands out in front of him. "Tamaya is getting older and soon she will pass down the drum to you. Tonight, you will fill in for her. Marie spoke so well of your performance last night. A flawless execution of the beat. You are ready, Aminata. Correct?"

"Yes, Elder Idrissa."

"Good. I will be checking in on some other people, but I will come and keep you company in a little while. I have so much faith in you, Aminata."

"Thank you, Elder Idrissa. I will not fail you."

"Take your seat and ready your drum. I will observe your start."

Aminata did as the elder instructed.

She followed the rhythm as soon as it came. Like the favorite memories stored in the fore of one's mind, she knew every beat before it hit and didn't miss one, sensing Idrissa's eyes on her. He didn't leave immediately, but waited until the beat repeated.

"Good, good, Aminata. You have it," he said. "I'll see you in a bit."

Aminata nodded.

She turned to make sure Idrissa had left, keeping the beat.

He was gone.

As she returned her gaze to the front, movement to the right alerted her senses. The boy stood behind one of the trees. He stared at her. He didn't move away as he had the previous night. Tingling, like static electricity, erupted within Aminata.

"Who are you?" Aminata asked.

The boy crooked his neck, surveying her from between two branches.

"I know you can hear me. Who are you? What tribe are you from? I've never seen you around here before last night."

The boy smiled.

"Talk to me."

The boy indicated for her to follow, before turning around and darting into the wilderness.

Aminata couldn't resist. She stopped playing and left the djembe drum at her feet. She looked around, making sure Idrissa wasn't watching her, and ran after the boy.

Either the jungle aided the boy or he had simply disappeared, as she couldn't locate him anywhere. Finding him in the world of towering trees and overgrown bush in the fading light would be near impossible. She stopped, clenching her fists as she conceded defeat. Looking to a section of low-growing bushes, she wished the boy would jump out and tell her who he was.

"Boy, if you can hear me, please come out."

She listened carefully, hoping a falling branch or snapping twig would give the boy away. Aminata heard nothing other than the usual jungle sounds. The drumbeat had gone quiet, yet it was still dusk. Maybe she was too far away to hear. The reassuring thuds and slaps were likely audible nearer to the village.

"Boy. I just want to talk to—"

Shouting came from behind her. She braced her back against an uninvited chill, as if someone had dumped icy water over her. Screams filled the atmosphere, and the usual jungle sounds went quiet. The shrieking cries were ones of pain and horror. Fear for her village replaced the curiosity for the boy; she ran back.

The screams hit a crescendo before fading out as she reached the spot with her djembe drum. She didn't stop, pushing through the burning in her lungs.

Nausea and dizziness rattled her as she entered her village.

The scene caused waves of heat to ride her skin.

The body parts of her fellow villagers had been hacked clean off. Their limbs lay scattered over the village, drenched in crimson blood. It was a massacre and she couldn't resist the gag reflex. She spewed vomit all over the earth as tears stung her eyes.

She steadied herself, first bracing against what fearful tribe or creatures had done this, but as she looked up, she realized night had come. The myth was true. The ghosts had brought forth this carnage. She wandered in a daze as her tears took forever to dry.

Willing herself into action, she identified the victims by collecting the decapitated heads with lifeless eyes and placed them in a pile near the center of the village. Her feet moved heavily and her hands shook, but she persevered, accounting for everyone, even Marie and Elder Idrissa.

The ghosts had spared no one.

Everyone she knew was dead.

She had done this. She'd failed to keep the beat.

Thoughts of fleeing entered her mind, but she canceled them. There could be no escape. She had to face the punishment for her failure. If only she'd believed the reasoning for the ritual as the rest of her tribe had. She took a seat in the middle of the village and stoked a dying fire.

Tomorrow, at dusk, her tribe would come for her.

There would be no beat to protect her.

BLOOD IS RED

Violet Sierra put her black bra on, while looking over the wrinkly, overweight, silver-haired man spread out on the rickety bed. The man, the town's police chief, exhaled a large cloud of smoke when he caught her gaze. In his left hand he held a cigarette, while his right arm remained handcuffed to the bed's headboard. His rotund stomach escaped coverage of the white bedsheet as he rubbed his feet together. The sound, like sandpaper against sandpaper, combined with the stench of sweat that hung in the room, threatening to test Violet's gag reflex. She loathed being around clients in the early-morning hours—or anytime during the day, but if they paid well, really well, she was prepared to suffer through it.

"So, I guess you heard about how Officer Bill and I caught that psycho from down south? You know, the one who was chopping up all those women with an ax. He wandered into our area and boom, we got him," the police chief said. "They called him Chop-chop."

"Yes, Harold, it was all over the news." Violet pulled her jeans up.

"What about how Officer Dickie and I caught that crazy-ass drug dealer last week? You know, that son of a bitch who was selling to the kids."

"Read about that as well."

"Oh, I see. What about—"

"Harold, I don't give a shit about what's happened," Violet said, raising her voice. She moved strands of hair out of her face. "You got your fuck. Now where is my money?"

"Well, about that." Harold tested the strength of the handcuffs. "I'll get it to you on Friday. I must be careful how I spend cash with the missus keeping sharp eyes on everything lately."

Violet walked toward him and slapped his bare chest.

Harold flinched. "Damn it. Was that necessary?"

"Yes. You cops are the worst fucking clients around. I don't want to see you until you have my money. That clear? No coming to the club unless you got it. And that goes for your buddies in blue as well, unless you want me to mention how you need a pill to get going."

"What the...? Don't be like that."

Violet gave Harold the middle finger.

"You girls, all mental. Can you at least unlock my handcuff now? I got to be at the office in a few."

"Go fuck yourself," Violet said, turning to grab her top.

She exited the room, ignoring Harold's cursing.

* * *

Violet viewed her naked, tanned, shapely physique in the mirror. Satisfied in her perfection, she reached for one of the white buckets at her feet. She lifted the bucket over her head, tilted it, and allowed the crimson substance to pour all over her. The splattering sounds the substance made as it hit the plastic beneath her feet electrified her within. Overwhelmed by this, and then the chemical odor that flooded her sense of smell, she had to lean forward and inhale deep, for fear of passing out.

"What the fuck is that?" Kelly, a newbie, said, entering the bathroom.

"It's blood."

"That's disgusting."

"It's just fake blood, chill."

Kelly held her hand in front of her mouth. "It still smells like shit. Oh-em-gee. Do you know what kind of freaks you're going to attract with a show like yours?"

"The freaks pay, sweetie. That's why you will always earn a tenth of what I do." Violet smiled. "I give the strange little sheep what they want, what they really want. The fire of your blonde locks and fake tits extinguishes very quickly."

"Oh, please," Kelly said. "Sex sells and I am the pinup girl of their dreams."

"Sex might sell, bitch," Violet said, giving Kelly the finger. "But freaky sex sells even better."

Violet left the bathroom and headed to the door leading to the stage. It was almost time for her last performance of the night, the main event. The lights were dimmed as the distant sounds of war drums played through the speakers. She tiptoed her way onto the darkened stage, barely able to see, but she could tell the place was packed by all the cigarette cherries that went red every time someone took a drag. When she felt the pole, she lay on her spot on the stage floor. There she pretended to be dead. It was easy, as she had done the pose so many times and not only on the stage.

She had worked at From Kittens to Panthers, the local strip club, for near on four years. There was no longer any doubt in her mind that she was the main attraction. Her heartbeat accelerated as she awaited her moment.

The announcer said, "Blood is red...and Violet is..."

"Dead!" the crowd shouted.

The lights came back on. A track heavy on bass boomed through the speakers, and like a phoenix rising from the ashes, Violet pulled herself up with the pole. She picked up a sponge at her feet as water sprinkled down from above.

She washed the blood off, slowly, as the crowd stared, mesmerized, at her ever more naked body. Money flew onto the stage like shrapnel flying around from an explosion.

Violet smiled. She could see the widened eyes that yearned for her, and the open mouths that drooled.

Here, she ruled.

She had no equal.

* * *

After her last show, Violet wandered around the patrons. They would all compliment her, and some would stick more bills into her black G-string as if they were trying to pin the tail on the donkey. There was a man sitting in one of the dimly lit corner booths, and he seemed oblivious to everything around him, including her.

Violet stalked toward him.

She sat with her rear on his table, giving him a view she doubted he could resist.

The man looked up. "Hi."

"Who the hell are you? You special?" Violet reached for his drink and swirled the brown liquid within.

"Me? I'm no one," the man said.

"I haven't seen you around here. Did you like the show?"

The man took back his whiskey and downed the contents. "I'm new to town, bit of an investor you could say. The show, well, it was okay. I've seen similar."

"Bullshit."

The man smiled. "What are you doing after work?"

"I'm already off. And as for what I'm doing, well, that depends on who has the deepest wallet," Violet said, looking around. There wasn't much hope, as most of the clientele were locals, and cheapskates when it came to the crunch. Added to this she had warned the chief from rocking up until he could clear his debts. She saw no other officers either. They were always good for a ride with a little bonus.

"I see," the man said, with no change in his expression.

"Where are you staying?" Violet indicated for a waitress walking by to bring them two drinks. Turning back to the man, she said, "You got this, right?"

"Sure. I'm staying outside of town in a little kind of cottage for now, think I saw a sign saying Baxter just before it. I'm still getting a feel for the place before I decide on something more permanent."

"Oh, I know the Baxter farm, used to be some crazy, weird parties there. You stay close by. I like that."

"Tell you what," the man said, "because you put so much effort into your show, I'll write down a number, and if you like it, we can head back to my place for a special repeat performance."

Violet chuckled. "Go on then."

The man took out a notepad and pen from his pocket. "Don't you want to know my name first?"

"Oh, if you need to say it, go ahead."

The man wrote on the piece of paper and slid the note to Violet. "Name's Mike."

Violet chuckled. "I'm sorry, Mike, but if you doubled this, you'd probably only be able to hammer one of the lower hanging fruits around here. I'm top shelf, do you understand?"

Violet turned to walk away.

"All right, all right. What if I triple it?"

"Mmm, that's better, much better. Come on then, let's get the fuck out of here."

* * *

Violet got out of Mike's vehicle and beheld the ramshackle cottage house. If it looked this beaten up at night, she wondered how dilapidated it might appear in the day. To say it needed some TLC would be an understatement, but that didn't matter. She had done it in trailers, cheap motel rooms, and even public restrooms. As long as they paid, they got laid.

She wandered over the front lawn, skipping over barren patches, then stared up at the sky. A chill in the air caused her to shudder, but a warmth in her chest grew as she pondered how much cash she could swindle out of the newcomer. He appeared hard up for sex, and that meant she could worm a few extra bills out of him.

Mike walked past her to the front door.

"You coming in?" Mike said, pushing open the creaking door.

"Don't you want to do it under the stars? Give the gods a show?"

"Ha," Mike said, rubbing the back of his neck. "Think the bed will be more comfortable."

"So boring." Violet followed him into the home.

Mike led her to the bedroom. "Want a beer?"

"You got anything stronger?"

"Tequila?"

Violet nodded.

After she had downed her second shot, Violet made her way to the bathroom to freshen up as Mike sat on the bed enjoying his beer. When she exited, wearing nothing but her black G-string, Mike stood in the far corner of the room. He had also changed his attire.

"What on earth are you wearing?"

Mike beamed, revealing rows of yellow-tinted teeth that had been hidden beneath a fake bushy red beard only a moment ago. "The beard? It's super comfortable."

"And the rest?"

Mike shrugged.

Violet walked toward him, looking him over. He wore a red-and-black checkered shirt with the sleeves rolled up, a brown beanie, dark denim trousers with black suspenders, a black belt fixed with various tools—including a hammer—and tan boots to round off his new appearance.

"Holy shit, you look like a damn lumberjack," she said. "Role-playing is extra, you little freak."

"It's not a role. I'm not a freak," Mike said. "This is the real me." He reached toward the side of the bed and lifted an ax. "See? Chop-chop."

"Chop-chop? Wait, wait, back the fuck up. What kind of sick game is this? You trying to reenact that crazy killer down south? This is how you get your kicks? I'm charging you five times my normal rate."

"That's a bit harsh." Mike frowned. "You know, I was going to just have a drink at your strip club and then carry on my way. When I heard they arrested the wrong guy, I knew I needed to move. But your show, you, your pain—well, sometimes I can't resist helping to free those who are in such devastating pain. And I want to set you free. Chop-chop."

"I'm not in pain, asshole." Violet stepped back. "I'm happy."

"Bullshit."

"This is too fucked. I'm going to go."

"Go? It's chop-chop time."

Violet couldn't help but recall what Kelly had said, how her show would attract the freaks. Maybe she should've toned down the spectacle a bit. Being a lightning rod for the weird—especially a guy who wanted to pretend he was a serial killer—no longer held the appeal it once did.

"You've had your fun." She looked for her clothes and handbag. "I'm leaving."

"You can't leave. I've got to set you free. Chop-chop," Mike said, swinging the ax through the air.

Violet regretted telling Chief Harold not to come around with his friends. If he or the officers had been there, it was likely this nutjob wouldn't have dared to misbehave.

Mike swung the ax again. This time he lost his grip and ended up tossing the tool into a lampshade in the corner of the room. "Damn. That's not chop-chop."

Violet had endured enough and bolted for the door.

She turned the handle, praying for the first time in ages.

An incredible force hit her square in the back as she realized that the door was locked—no quick escape. She braced as her chest slammed against the door. A searing pain erupted between her shoulder blades as disorientation in the form of dizziness reigned. She turned around, glancing to see blood running down the back of her left calf.

Mike held the ax. There was blood dripping from its blade.

"You...you hit me." Violet struggled to keep her balance. Her pulse pounded where she had been struck. It occurred to her that Mike might not be role-playing after all. That dumb shit Chief Harold had apprehended the wrong person.

Mike grabbed her right arm and flung her back into the room. She toppled onto the ground, then got to her knees, hoping she could crawl and escape. The pain in her back now burned like mature hellfire. "Please, please just stop. I don't want to die."

"I'm setting you free," Mike said. "Chop-chop."

"Please, I don't—"

Mike brought the ax down on her left hand, severing her index and middle fingers, while severely wounding her ring finger and pinky. Blood spurted out the new wounds.

Violet screamed.

Adrenaline pumped, but it wasn't enough to temporarily stifle the pain and give her a boost for a last chance at escape. She fell flat. Rage had replaced her desire for mercy. "Fuck you. You freak. Fuck. Freak. You," she managed to get out.

Violet attempted to lift her gaze from the dirty carpet to get a look at Mike—hoping he had vanished. Her vision was blurry, but it cleared enough to see that he was still standing there. He had raised the ax above his head.

"What did the announcer say again before your show?" Mike asked.

Violet grunted.

"Oh, now I remember. Blood is red and Violet is..."

NEW SKULLS FOR THE OLD CEMETERY

The heavens resembled the remains of a fire. The dark tones, from ashy gray to starless-sky black, were an augur to the coming storm, but worries of rain, wind, and lightning had to take a back seat for now. James Brady's moment had arrived. Having lured two of his best friends to the cemetery, he could proceed with his idea. He hoped they would never know it was the only reason he had asked them to take up the ruse of adventure.

The tingling combination of fear and excitement that ran internally, like an electric current through water, as they traversed the realm of the dead had been the perfect precursor for the game. This was his master plan. This was his time. In a moment of inspiration and genius, he had devised the game only a few days before.

It would not fail.

Then, the girl he'd had a crush on for two years, Michelle, threw his life a curveball.

"Instead of me kissing you if the dice lands on an even number," she said, "why don't you both throw the dice and the highest wins the kiss? That way there's guaranteed to be a winner."

Fuck.

Shit.

The punch to James' gut was worse than the time he had taken a baseball to the stomach. He wanted to curse out loud and had to grind his teeth to prevent any words from escaping. He didn't enjoy leaving things to chance, especially the potential of kissing Michelle. Her soft pink lips were often front of mind, ever since the day he first met her in math class. Everything about her mesmerized. From the way she spoke, confident and eloquent, to the way her straight blonde hair glowed when hit by rays of the sun.

"That's a great idea." Louis grinned.

Yanked back to the present, James considered exchanging the rigged die—made to land only on even numbers—for the regular one in his pocket. He also wanted to kick his friend's head off like a placekicker slotting over a field goal. Surely, Louis must've had an inkling of his crush on Michelle. He had never told him, but they were best friends, and best friends should sense important things.

Louis stepped forward. "I'll go first—"

"No," James said, giving his friend some side-eye. "I'll go first."

He had resisted the urge to swap the dice, not wanting them to discover his plan, and tossed the one in his hand into the air.

It came back down, then landed on the dirt at their feet.

Four.

James was indifferent. He had hoped for a six, but it was better than a two. Once more, he considered changing the dice out, but the backstabber, Louis, swooped and picked up the die before he could continue with the idea.

"Well, well," Louis said. "It was an even number. If this weren't a two-person challenge, you'd have gotten a kiss. Guess I'm in luck."

Michelle patted him on the arm. "Ha. Don't be so overconfident. You still might lose."

"Lose? Me? Never."

James wanted to drive a fist through Louis' face, like a boxer landing a knockout blow, but instead, all he did was force a smile.

"Here we go, baby." Louis tossed the die high into the air.

It bounced on a rock as it returned to earth, and then it spun next to a small branch, which covered the die from the three friends' line of sight.

James stepped closer.

Six.

"Woo-hoo!" Louis hollered behind him.

By the time James turned back to his friends, Louis had his arm around Michelle's waist. Their lips locked as their tongues swapped saliva. The smacking sounds caused fire to rage within James' stomach, as if hell had manifested within him. Louis rubbed his hand over Michelle's chest, cupping her right breast.

She moved his hand. "That's enough, for now."

"Sure." Louis smiled. He looked to James. "Thanks for the great idea, James. I owe you one, buddy."

"Fuck both of you," James said. The urge to rip Louis' head off his shoulders ignited inside of him, but he doused the idea. That was madness. Maybe he should beat the shit out of Louis instead, until he was nothing more than a skin bag of pulp and broken bones. That was a saner plan.

"Excuse me?" Michelle's eyes narrowed as she pointed at him. "You don't talk to me like that."

"Yeah, man," Louis said. "That's uncalled for."

"I will fucking say what I fucking want."

A look of cold disappointment invaded Michelle's usually soft and warm face. The desire to beat Louis up dissipated as if it were cigarette smoke in the wind. Still, he didn't have to stand here like a fool, embarrassed and crushed.

"It was only a game. Your game," Louis said. "You should apologize."

James threw them both zap signs before turning around and strutting off.

Louis called after him.

He ignored the desire to tell his false friend to go fuck himself.

Heading deeper into the cemetery, he decided he no longer had time for shit in his life, especially when it came to fake friends. Did he truly like Michelle that much anyway? He couldn't recall as he clenched his fists at his sides.

He pulled the spare die from his pocket and tossed it against a gravestone up ahead, mumbling, "Stupid fucking game."

A chill in the air compounded the internal battle of bitterness and loss. No matter how hard he stomped, he couldn't vanquish the emotions. Anger remained somewhere inside as well, teasing him periodically with its heat. He placed his hands in his jacket's pockets, walking faster to warm himself.

Pink and purple shades streaked across the dark clouds overhead.

Nightfall had come.

* * *

The cemetery was one of the oldest in the county, and it showed. James traversed field upon field filled with generic headstones and the odd more lavish gravestone. How many buried corpses were there? There appeared to be many. The stone path he followed narrowed and changed to a simple dirt path. Even the grass here was longer, and the trees wilder, as their branches hung over the path. He couldn't imagine how difficult the upkeep of such a place must be. Or was it really that big? When he rode his bike past it during the day, it didn't seem as expansive. Were the night and his feelings deceiving him?

He came upon an ancient section of the cemetery surrounded by knee-high black fencing. The graves all shared the same small rectangular headstones, but one stood out. It had a white angel statue placed atop it, reflecting the now blue-and-green colors in the otherwise black cloudy sky. The wind had also strengthened, but it wasn't powerful enough to pierce his sports jacket.

James hopped off the path, stepped over the fencing, and walked over a few graves en route to the special headstone.

The angel came loose when he grabbed it.

"Cool," James said, tossing it into the air and catching it as he would a baseball. The size was in fact similar to a baseball, and he considered pitching as if it were one, but he stopped himself. Maybe he would take it for a keepsake instead. His father had once gotten inebriated after his mother's death and had remarked she wouldn't make a useful angel, as she'd never made a useful housewife. James had wanted to smash one of the empty beer bottles littering the living room over his father's head. Maybe he would keep the angel to throw at his old man when he mentioned his mother again.

Making his way back to the path, he discovered it wasn't an area as forgotten as he had initially assumed. There was an empty grave less than twenty yards to his right.

"How bizarre," James said, marching to the pile of dirt alongside the hole.

He kicked at the soil, figuring someone had dug the grave recently. As he looked around, all he saw was the lifeless cemetery. The fear of a groundskeeper being in the area faded.

Bored, he searched for something to occupy his mind, but all he had was the angel he held. Why keep it anyway? To remember this shitty night?

"Fuck that." He flung the angel high into the air, as if he were taking a three-point shot, aiming for the empty grave.

It landed with a *thud* but didn't break.

"Damn it."

He wanted to retrieve the angel, so he could destroy it properly, but resisted. The idea of getting stuck in the six-foot hole wasn't a pleasant one. His thoughts returned to his friends, and his stomach turned. The anger from earlier resurfaced as fast as flicking a switch to light a room. He picked up a few stones at his feet and tossed them at whichever gravestones drew his attention.

Something new caught his eye.

It was a vase filled with flowers, placed on an otherwise standard headstone. He now had the perfect target at which to unleash the rocks. Picking out the largest stone in his hand, he grinned.

Steadying himself, he imagined himself to be a pitcher in a World Series game. It was the bottom of the ninth—another strike and his team would be champions.

"I wouldn't do that," a man with a rough voice said from behind him.

Drizzle patted his head and shoulders.

The rain had arrived.

* * *

Once, when James was younger, his father had denied him a treat at their local store. This wasn't long after his mother passed. She had rolled the family car on an icy road after heading out late one evening to buy ingredients she lacked for dinner. His mother had first asked his father to go, but he'd declined, as he was too busy watching television. The memory hurt like touching a hot stove. One memory that soothed, however, was that his mother bought him a little treat whenever they went shopping together. So, when his father said "no" during their first trip to the store after her passing, the word echoed in his mind like a chainsaw cutting metal. Unable to accept the answer, he had waited for his father to turn away and slipped a chocolate bar into his jacket pocket.

It didn't matter what he selected.

All that mattered was he took a treat.

His father had caught him, however, having turned back with ninja-like reflexes. Being lectured and punished by his father for stealing was embarrassing at first, but the humiliation had turned slowly to anger. This led him to hide his father's keys a week later, causing his old man to be late for an important work meeting.

Hearing the voice behind him in the cemetery, he went from embarrassment to anger in record time. Who was this person telling him what he could or couldn't do?

James turned around, ready to retaliate.

An old man stood, leaning with his right shoulder against a tree near the path. He looked homeless with his large tattered brown coat flapping in the breeze and wild silver-gray hair that hung to his shoulders. His beard was near white and had won the war against his wrinkled face. The man held a spade in front of him.

"Who the fuck are you?" James asked.

"I dig the graves."

"Great. You'll have to just deal with my mess." James licked his lips. It was time for the vase's destruction.

The gravedigger shook his head. "Nope. That would be work for the groundskeeper and his staff. They only come during the day. I dig graves at night. We never see each other."

"So why do you give a shit what I do? Why disturb me?"

"Because," the gravedigger said, spreading out his arms, "this is my home. I live here."

"In the cemetery? That's fucked up, bro. Where's your house?"

The gravedigger frowned. He stumbled forward, using the spade as a cane. "You're not pleasant, you know? People should have good manners around the dead. But, to answer your question, sometimes you can see my house and sometimes you can't. Depends on my mood."

"That's funny. If you think you're going to spook me, you're wrong, and as for the dead, well, they're dead. They don't give a shit." James had grown tired of the back and forth, and he tossed one of the rocks at the vase.

The vase shattered and dropped to the earth, in pieces.

The flowers fell around the shards.

Thunder rumbled. A crack of lightning lit up the sky.

"That was unfortunate," the gravedigger sneered. His eyes narrowed, and the wrinkles on his face had magically smoothed as if whatever he felt within didn't adhere to the wear and tear of years gone by. It could've been an illusion in the poor light, though. "Yes, that was a dreadful thing to do."

James wanted to curse and show the gravedigger a middle finger, but he didn't want to waste any more time. He turned and strode to the path, unable to resist throwing his hand up at the man as if shooing away a fly.

"I'm in a good mood. Even though you did that," the gravedigger said.

James stopped and looked back. This wasn't a night anyone deserved to feel good. "Oh yeah? And why's that?"

"Some people were buried today."

"Man, you have issues."

"Tell you what, kid. You apologize for what you did. Clean up, and I'll let it slide. I mean, it couldn't have been fun watching the pretty girl kissing the other boy."

"You were spying on us? You creep."

The gravedigger chuckled. "I see all in the cemetery. In fact, another man has entered this domain. He's got a bottle of liquor with him. I do hope he behaves tonight. I'd hate to have to dig more graves."

"Man, stop trying to frighten me. What are you—drunk? Fuck's sake. Kiss my ass, you old loser." James marched his way to the path.

The gravedigger whistled.

This time James ignored him.

Rustling came from the trees to his left. James had to listen carefully with the constant drizzle and the thunder roaring periodically. The rustling sound came again, louder than before. Something approached, and James looked back.

The gravedigger had vanished.

The rain came down harder.

"Fuck this shit." James accelerated forward until he broke into an all-out sprint. He told himself he wasn't scared, but that he had been in the cemetery long enough.

When he arrived back at the stone path, his frayed nerves calmed, even though he had to watch his footing for fear of slipping.

Red streaks now infected the dark clouds overhead. The storm was turning into the weirdest he had encountered, but soon he'd be out of the cemetery, and eventually he would be home.

After a while, he slowed to a jog. Why wasn't he already near the entrance? Something wasn't right. The trees all looked alike. The headstones once again shared a generic design. In fact, he couldn't spot any unique ones.

He upped his pace again.

A dark shape sprung out from behind one of the trees to his right. He didn't turn to get a look, opting to focus ahead and where his feet landed next. Something impacted him, something big, and he was knocked onto the ground.

He pushed himself onto his knees.

Winded, he focused, searching for whatever had attacked him. Fortunately, it appeared to have come and gone. He settled on it being a random lost animal. His mind cemented the idea. Yes, merely a dumb animal. He could still smell the stench of the... Maybe it was a dog. If it was a dog, it was a big one.

He stood, making sure nothing moved behind any of the trees. When he was sure it was clear, he'd dash off again. The cemetery exit was all he could think of as he surveyed the world around him.

The dark shape appeared ahead, blocking his path.

"Fuck," he said, seeking another direction for escape.

He found no way other than having to traverse more areas filled with gravestones. Looking again, the shape had formed into that of a dog. Surely the transformation was another illusion brought on by the rush of adrenaline. His first assumption that it was a big dog had been correct, however.

The dog had prickly black hair, and on all fours, it was at least waist-high to James. Its eyes flashed red, but it was not alone. The gravedigger stood next to it, running his hand over the animal's back.

"All right," James said, holding his hands up. "You had your fun, old man. Now let me get the fuck out of here."

"I'm afraid that's no longer a possibility. You've disturbed the dead. I can't appear weak and allow you to simply waltz out of here. You desecrated graves and have no respect for this realm."

"Fucking let me go, you nut, or I'll call the—" James checked his pocket, then realized he'd given his cell to Louis to make a call after his friend's phone had died. That had been before they'd entered the cemetery. Louis, the dumb son of a bitch, hadn't returned the phone.

The gravedigger whistled.

The dog leaped forward, headed straight for James.

It came fast. Paws with sharp nails pushed into James' chest, sending him backward. The impact was impressive, and the animal's stench invaded his sense of smell. It would be his end, if he fell over. He fought to keep his balance, managing for a moment, but the force, the power, was too much to withstand as the animal pounced again.

James landed on his rear, hard.

Searing pain exploded over his right shoulder. An uncomfortable heat followed the harrowing sensation of flesh being torn from his body.

The fucking dog had bitten him.

He held his right hand out to protect his face, and the dog nipped off two of his fingers. One moment the digits were there and the next they were gone. Blood spurted across his view, burning his eyes. The pain erupted from everywhere.

"It's eating me! It's eating me!"

The old man whistled.

The dog ceased its attack.

Delirium had taken over; James lay back and searched for clarity as the gravedigger kneeled beside him with his shovel. He wanted to curse the man, but something was wrong. Empty space existed where the surface of his neck should've been. He lowered his hand further, touching a mess reminding him of spaghetti drenched in sauce.

The gravedigger smiled. "Don't worry, kid. Your friends left the cemetery a little while back. They were holding hands. Isn't that sweet?"

James gurgled.

"A new skull is always welcome, possibly two. The other man has thrown his empty bottle at one of the gravestones. The dead speak. They're not happy." The gravedigger ran his hand over James' forehead. "There is always room for new skulls in the old cemetery."

James couldn't breathe.

His chest burned as if doused in gasoline and set ablaze.

The gravedigger stood.

He raised the spade with the sharp, curved shoveling side aimed for what remained of James' throat.

James looked up, seeing the stars above.

The storm had passed.

COUNTDOWN TO EXTINCTION

I sat under an artificial rock formation, waiting for the clouds overhead to pass. The desaturated and somber tones of the world around me were a reflection of my mind. Even the rhythmic patter of the rain no longer soothed. I adjusted the name tag pinned onto my white coat.

One can still look respectable.

Doctor Aleem Bhatnagar, leaning against a *real* tree with his slender frame, indicated at something with his deep-set brown eyes.

"It's raining," I said, not bothering to look.

"Come now, it's only a few drops." His lips moved in the nest of his wild black beard. His name tag dangled askew on his dirtied white coat.

I scratched my own beard, which like my wild shoulder-length hair, was gray. I breathed in deep. The smell of falling rain flooded my senses.

"God's sake, Mike, look."

"It's Doctor Alberts...or Mychal."

"Okay, just look at this."

"Fine." I stood; the bones of my thin body creaked. The rain ceased, and I found no change of emotion within myself as I shuffled over to him. His demonstrating became more animated, and reluctantly I looked to where he pointed.

Beyond the steel bars of the enclosure, on a dark wooden bench, sat Rubik, our only koala. His round fluffy ears and silver-gray pelage stayed dry under a red-and-white striped umbrella behind him. Thanks to us, his once-weak respiratory system was now a memory of the past.

"So? Should I be surprised he's awake for once?"

"In his hands," Aleem whispered.

I couldn't see the reason for the dialed-down volume, since Rubik was impervious to our actions. I actively stared at Rubik to pacify Aleem. "He's using the touch-screen analytics pad. What's your point?"

"I think he recalibrated it. He was fiddling at the back."

"You're imagining that."

"No—"

"Impossible. They can't advance so fast."

"Oh, and what of the repair work we taught them?" Aleem's eyes strained, accentuating the wrinkles on his dark-skinned face.

"So, a few of the animals learned to do minor repair work? Nuts-and-bolts nonsense. You're suggesting a different level of understanding."

Aleem didn't reply. His attention returned to Rubik. *Can they be advancing that fast?*

I tried to drown out the thought as I made my way to the steel bars of the enclosure. I gripped the bars; the cold surface numbed my hands.

Our parent company, the Eisenberg CyTech Corporation, had funded our research. The artificial body parts and organs, barring the brain, that we'd developed had made them a leading force in the global economy. In return, they handed us the freedom to pursue our experiments into the unknown.

It was the BAO3X chip that would become the pinnacle of our work, our magnum opus, as Aleem used to love saying. The aim of the neural implant, in the form of our chip, was basic. We channeled what we deemed unnecessary brain-energy wastage so we could stimulate areas of the brain known for learning and development. The brain, however, is not simple. Our efforts would not be without trial and error, and this would be where we encountered our first true hurdle, one the green in the pockets of the Eisenberg CyTech Corporation could not buy over.

After we'd formulated tests for our prototype, the bureaucratic red tape unrolled, halting our progress, all human trials denied. A think tank would point out the alternative...animals. "It's what they're there for," a former colleague at the time joked.

I turned my back to the bite in the wind and looked at my silver wristwatch—an heirloom passed down to me by my father—the moving silver second hand hypnotic. Its design was simple: the hands moved over the white clock face and silver numbers, with the digital time below, where I would set the alarm. A feature I'd come to abhor.

"Hey, Merc," Aleem said.

"No, leave Brad," I said.

The monosyllabic Brad Mercer, our head of security, operated in a perpetual bad mood. I held my breath as I glanced at him; he had his back to us. His dirty-blond hair touched his broad shoulders, and the white shirt he wore was so badly faded it was nearly transparent.

He didn't move.

I exhaled.

Aleem asked, "Is it lunch?"

I tensed. "No, not yet." I forced my eyes away from my wristwatch. My skin crawled as I recalled how Aleem could snap during feeding times. It was safer to observe Rubik.

We'd packed up operations on the west coast of America and moved our facilities to our current location in eastern Germany, which was our founder and majority shareholder Janusz Eisenberg's homeland.

Our new project ran under the guise of the Eisenberg CyTech New Age Zoo. We'd built immaculate enclosures for the animals we rescued, or procured by other means. People would come in and marvel at how we'd saved the lives of the array of animals on display.

For a while we had been heroes.

Behind the scenes we studied the effects of the chips we'd implanted in the brains of the animals. I hadn't been as enthusiastic to test on animals. Aleem, however, became enthralled, and would rattle off facts on animals with machine-gun-like fire.

Those days had passed. Now I could hear the undertone in his voice, the fear unmistakable. I recalled the same undertone in my mother's voice when she'd called to tell me my father had died. That was a week after I'd arrived in Germany. The wristwatch I now wore had arrived in the mail not too long after. Maybe its purpose was to serve as a reminder of fear, the fear in my mother's voice, and at times in Aleem's, and now in my own.

Teet, teet... Teet, teet.

The sound of the wristwatch echoed around us, yanking me from my thoughts. The color on Aleem's face drained. He scurried to the bars of our enclosure and banged on them.

"It's lunchtime, you bastards. Come on!"

"Doctor Bhatnagar, all you're going to do is anger them. Please calm down." I held out my hands before me, mimicking a mime stuck in a box.

Aleem ignored me. He picked up a branch he'd sharpened on the concrete floor. With this he banged on the bars. Feeding times turned Aleem into this animal, and I didn't know how to stop it. I feared it was the road all three of us would eventually end up on. I flinched as a frigid breeze embraced me.

A door cracked open, and a chimpanzee came out from the green building to our right. He was pushing a cardboard box full of assorted fruit—bananas and oranges primarily—and bottles of water. I guessed the bananas were a bit of irony aimed at us.

Fucking bananas.

He left the box a step from our enclosure. A citrus aroma teased my sense of smell.

Aleem calmed, made his way to the bars, and dragged the box closer with his branch. He took out the water and the fruit, placing everything in a pile beside him.

Another chimpanzee came knuckle-walking out of the building, and he joined the first. He stood and moved his hands as if communicating with the other. It reminded me of sign language mixed with the movements of an artist painting, only here there was no paint, brush, or easel, only strokes with his finger. He made a turning motion with his hand, as if he were unscrewing an imaginary bottle cap. The other chimpanzee nodded along.

How strange.

"It's a code."

I turned to see Brad grab one of the bananas Aleem had retrieved from the box. His face was as bland and hardened as ever, but his light beard was graying at its ends. He narrowed his dark-blue eyes at the two chimpanzees.

"Code?" I said.

"Yes."

"Why not their normal vocalization?"

"Basic universal gestures, so they and other animals can understand orders." Brad spoke as softly as he could without whispering.

"What other animals?"

"All other animals."

"Orders from whom?"

"I think the primates are only workers, doing chores, relaying messages—"

"Orders from whom?" I repeated.

Brad didn't reply. I watched him turn and head back to his usual spot, where he sat on one of the artificial rocks, still facing us.

The second chimpanzee showed a symbol with his hands—unseen to me—to Rubik, who climbed off the bench. The two chimpanzees turned and headed back to the green building. Rubik, with the analytics pad gripped in his mouth, was a few steps behind.

Aleem had collected all the fruit and water. He was himself again, whatever that meant.

He pulled out a piece of red crayon from the top pocket of his coat and made his way to a flat surface on one of the rock formation's walls. He drew a horizontal line, which added to all the other red strokes over the surface of the fake rock. We'd circle the lines, always in groups of five, once we hit five.

"That's eighty-six," Aleem said. "Day fucking eighty-six."

I didn't reply. Neither did Brad, who stared into the distance as he chewed on the faintly green banana.

Eighty-six days ago, when the animals had escaped their confines and revolted, the three of us had locked ourselves in this enclosure. We thought it would be the best way to survive until help arrived.

* * *

Day eighty-seven came, and beams of faint sunlight broke through the clouds.

Later, the green building's door screeched open. I jolted from the sudden break in the lull of activity around me. Aleem moved to the bars of our enclosure. I joined him as my heartbeat gained momentum.

"*Pongo pygmaeus*, the Bornean orangutan," Aleem said.

I peered over his shoulder. An orangutan with its unmistakable reddish-brown hair was walking toward us. The titanium alloy endoskeleton arm on his right side, encasing the electrodes and other mechanical parts, shone silver even under the fading light. The hair on the base of my neck stood. I'd named him Smiley, for when he had arrived, he'd answer any questions by curling his top lip, exposing his yellow teeth. He'd lost his right arm in a fight in the wild, or at least that was the story given to us.

We'd attached the artificial arm to the stump below his shoulder, but for many days it dangled limp at his side. Once we inserted the chip, everything changed, and within weeks you would've sworn he'd been born with it. The eerie part came when he favored it. We never got around to covering the endoskeleton of the arm with synthetic skin and fur, but I no longer carried any guilt.

"What does Smiley want?" Aleem asked.

"I'm not sure." I turned to Brad, who was unmoved, and back to facing the opposite direction.

Smiley stopped in front of us. He raised his artificial arm along with his left arm and pulled at the hairs of his chest, reminding me of a blue-collar worker pressing on the straps of his overalls with his thumbs.

"Do you know what he wants?" Aleem's gaze remained fixed on Smiley.

"You're the animal expert."

Smiley pointed at me and repeated the action of pulling the hair on his chest.

"I'm stumped." Aleem rubbed his forehead.

Smiley waved his hand at the building. A bird flew out the door, which stood ajar, and came straight for him. It found a resting spot on his left shoulder.

Rain started to fall, softly.

Smiley was unmoved.

"How'd he call the bird?" I asked.

"I don't know," Aleem said. His face was full of intrigue. I knew my face would mirror his.

"What bird is that?"

"*Psittacus erithacus*, the African grey parrot. It must've been in the bird enclosure, although I don't remember us having any of that species."

"Me either."

The parrot's charcoal-gray feathers shimmered under the drops of rain. Something odd stood out. A chill pierced my chest. I looked at Aleem, who stared back at me.

"The right eye, you see that?"

"Yes," he whispered.

The parrot's right eye was black with a red light in its center. It moved from left to right, surely mechanical, resembling an archaic spy camera. Was it scanning us? Or recording maybe? The eye's movement reminded me of that of an animatronic triceratops I'd seen in an amusement park as a child.

This is nonsense. You're losing it.

Smiley pointed at me again. Once more he lifted his arms to his chest and repeated the pulling-of-his-hair action.

"What does—"

"Your coat, please," the parrot said.

My body tensed. I turned to Aleem.

"Am I going mad?"

"Non compos mentis, and nope, I heard it too."

"Your coat, please," the parrot repeated in its flat-toned voice.

"Give it to him. See what he does," Aleem said.

My body was frozen. A bout of nausea hit me as I dared to entertain the prospect of surrendering my coat.

"No."

"Why not?"

"Give him yours, if you want."

Aleem took off his coat, which was dirtier than mine. Gingerly, he stepped to the bars of the enclosure and passed the coat through. Smiley accepted it. He cast a disapproving eye at me—I stood firm—and he waved his hand.

"Thank you," the parrot said to Aleem.

It took off again, heading for the building.

Smiley flapped the coat out and did something that triggered an ominous pulling within my stomach. He put on the coat. Neither I nor Aleem said anything.

The coat was far too big for Smiley; it seemed he'd drown in the white material. But he rolled up the sleeves, which helped a bit, the bottom of the coat still dragging on the floor as he turned and headed for the building. He disappeared inside, and the door closed.

"Clever bastards."

I turned; Brad was facing us.

"How'd the parrot know what to ask?" Aleem asked.

"Must've been taught," I said.

Brad stood. "They use the birds for surveillance. You see the eye? They send 'em out, record—"

"Whoa, we don't know that for sure."

Brad said nothing further. I shrugged. I'd seen the eye, but managed to coax my mind into disbelief. Aleem, with his mouth hanging open, wanted to speak. My watch stopped him.

Teet, teet... Teet, teet.

The pandemonium of lunch followed.

* * *

Night came. I tried to close my eyes while lying on the real grass in the enclosure; it was still uncomfortable, no matter how long it grew.

The day the animals had launched their coup, we'd managed to lock ourselves in our cage. Harrowing screams from the zoo's employees and visitors filled the air for a good thirty minutes, and then silence.

The zoo had kept chimpanzees and other primates initially. They were intelligent and the best suited for our data collection, but they disappointed. We decided to test others. First animals of the nearby areas: gray wolves and red foxes. Then came a few tigers, lions, and whatever came our way, including an African elephant that had suffered irreparable damage to his trunk. The artificial replacement we'd made had truly been a remarkable feat.

Near the end we'd even experimented on birds—mostly white-tailed eagles frequent in the area—in a specially designed enclosure for them. We had implanted all these animals with the BA03X chip. And they were now free.

A week after that first horrific day came the explosions. We could hear them all around the neighboring areas of the zoo. Brad said it'd been strategic. I'd built a wall in my mind to shut out such ideas. It'd been at this point Brad seemed to withdraw. Aleem and I didn't want to give up hope these events had been isolated and soon we would be free. To have believed otherwise would've brought the wall crashing down, leaving only guilt and despair.

I folded my arms, rubbing my shoulders. The nights were becoming colder.

Why had they left us be in the enclosure? Even given us food and water?

It may've been because we'd been their facilitators. The three of us had been in charge. We were involved in every decision, each step. Brad and his security team had kept a watchful eye as Aleem and our team continued to experiment. Maybe it was simpler; we were no longer a threat.

"It's as if they're at war."

Brad's voice pulled me from my thoughts. I sat up. The bright standing lights outside our enclosure illuminated us. Brad had once said they'd switched on the lights at night to observe us. While I couldn't eradicate the notion, I'd managed to avoid overanalyzing it.

Brad, seated a few feet from me, crossed his legs.

I decided to hear him out. "A war with what?"

"They've been building their numbers. You two have even said you've noticed animals that were never part of the zoo." Brad's cold gaze shifted between me and Aleem, who'd joined us.

"We have organized militaries... There's no chance," I said.

"They had the element of surprise. Only the corporation truly knows what we've been doing, and even they don't truly comprehend the power of the chips."

"This is true." Aleem's voice quivered.

I had the urge to slap him for jumping on the bandwagon. I didn't.

"I've noticed things." Brad stood, looking around. Satisfied, he kneeled closer to us.

"Like what?" I asked. Cracks were appearing in the wall in my mind.

"The day of the explosions... Well, to put it bluntly, I saw white-tailed eagles with strange metal balls in their talons. I'm confident they were explosives."

"Why didn't you say anything?"

"What could we do? We're locked in here. We don't even know what they changed our enclosure code to."

"I can't see how a few animals could take on the world."

"I know it seems primitive, but think; you have given them these advanced brain abilities. And if you add this to their number one instinct—"

"Survival." Aleem's eyes widened.

"Exactly. They see human beings as the threat—the way we pollute, kill, destroy. We've given them a way to communicate with each other, essentially handing them the power to take back the world."

I shuddered. The word "communication" danced in my mind.

"That was the explosions we heard... Sabotage. I'm guessing they've already advanced to the point where they're able to replicate the chips and have spread them worldwide. I know I'm not a science guy, but you said the operation to insert the chips wasn't that intrusive. Hell, you guys said machines made the chips and other machines did the surgery. How many animals could they have inserted with chips before anyone even knew?"

My insides knotted. "I can't believe that a bunch of fucking animals—"

"Wait," Aleem interrupted. "All the computers and machines are set up. If they've taken over the operations room, it's true what Brad says. It wouldn't be so hard to keep producing chips, parts." Aleem paused, rubbing his index finger over his cracked lips. "And remember, Rubik, the *Phascolarctos cinereus*—"

"Koala, Aleem. Shit, stop with the Latin," I said. Guilt hit my core. Naming the animals, the way he'd learned, was a way for him to deal with his situation. "Sorry, continue."

"W-well, the koala, Rubik, was working on the analytics pad. What Brad is saying... Shit, Mychal, I could believe it. You know how far they'd advanced up until... Well, you know."

Up until everything went to shit.

"I just—"

A loud *creak* ended our meeting. It was a sound I knew but hadn't heard in a while. I turned to the right, and the black steel gates, locked for the past eighty-seven days, were opening. There was another *creak*. This one, to our left, sustained longer. The black steel gates on the far left were now opening as well.

Aleem, Brad, and I got to our feet. We made our way to the bars of our enclosure, less than a step from the paved path between the two gates on our sides.

"What's going on?" Aleem asked. "Are...are we being saved?"

The word "saved" lingered. It took me awhile to understand what it meant. A surge of warmth exploded in my chest as I tried to see what was going on.

Time slowed as we waited to see what came next.

* * *

"No rescue. It's them," Brad said.

"Fuck!" I shouted.

"Calm down."

The three of us imitated statues as we watched the scene unfold. Chimpanzees on either side opened the gates and stood aside. From the right came two rows of red foxes, their reddish-brown fur visible under the tall standing lights of the zoo. They walked side by side, at a unified tempo, marching.

Rubik exited the building. He went and stood ahead of the foxes, right by our enclosure, the analytics pad in hand. My throat tightened. The foxes paused before him as he made a circle sign with his paw. He followed the action with three short dashes. The fox in front lifted its paw and drew a circle.

The foxes resumed their march. It was Brad who first became animated, and he made his way to Rubik, who had his back to us.

"No!" I screamed.

Aleem gasped.

Brad reached over Rubik and snatched the analytics pad from him. Rubik turned around, his eyes frozen in a state of shock. *How dare you human beings?* I imagined he thought. He took a few steps back, putting the foxes between himself and our enclosure.

"Check...check here." Brad's voice wavered, breaking from the adrenaline that must've pumped through his body.

I looked at the analytics pad's screen. My heart threatened to explode. I sensed Aleem looking over my shoulder.

"Target Berlin," he said.

"I see it," I said.

"I told you guys... Holy shit." Brad clenched his fists.

"Shit. We need to—"

Brad swooped down and picked up the branch on the floor—which Aleem used to get the box of fruit and water—and headed for the foxes marching right outside our enclosure.

"Don't!" I shouted.

Brad stuck the branch through the steel bars, the nearest fox his target.

The aim was pure, and the branch stuck into the side of the fox. It didn't flinch. The sharpened branch ripped the skin and fur off the animal. There was no blood. The rip did expose something else.

"Fuck," Brad said.

Aleem was dead quiet, and as pale as freshly fallen snow.

It'd been a type of armor beneath the reattached layers of skin, built from scrap metal. The makeshift material didn't take away from the fact that not only were the animals enhanced with our chips, but also with artificial parts—not of our design. The realization flooded me. Brad and Aleem's fears were true. The wall in my mind came crashing down.

Rubik shook his head. There was something ominous to his slow movements. He turned and headed back to the building. The flow of foxes ended. Four dozen had passed us.

Aleem was looking over the analytics pad. His face had accelerated to old age. "What are we going to do?"

"What can we do?" I asked.

Brad said nothing.

Aleem and I sat in silence.

Brad walked in circles, mumbling to himself.

Half an hour passed. Smiley emerged from the darkness of the building door, which stood ajar, the African grey parrot on his shoulder. He made his way to us. The head of a tiger appeared from the shadows behind him.

Aleem gasped as the rest of the tiger's body entered the lights, if you could call it a body. It was primarily mechanical. There was no skin, no fur, no bone, no muscle. It seemed all that remained were the major organs encased and protected by strange metallic cages. The *clang* sounds the tiger made as its feet hit the paved path were unnerving.

I stepped back. Brad and Aleem did the same. Smiley continued to our enclosure's gate and stopped, the tiger lurking a step behind. Smiley paused with his hand over the keypad and looked at us. None of us moved. We had no escape. Aleem prayed under his breath.

"I'm sorry it came to this," the parrot said.

Smiley nodded along.

"To w-what?" I asked.

Brad stepped forward, pressing his hand against my chest, guiding me back. He was readying himself for whatever came his way. He crouched.

"I can appreciate what you've done for us," the parrot said.

Smiley looked away.

The parrot continued, "Unfortunately, I'm not the one in command."

"Who's in charge?" Brad asked.

"The one you named Fred."

"Fred! The elephant, but—"

"Shhh," Brad said, interrupting Aleem. "How far have you spread?"

"Everywhere."

"Are you at war?"

"Unable to reply."

"What are your plans?"

"Unable to reply."

"Fuck, answer me!" Brad shouted.

"Thank you for helping us reclaim our beloved earth. I'm sorry it came to this. You must understand it has to be done. Goodbye, saviors."

The parrot took flight.

A despondent Smiley entered the code. Our enclosure's gate opened, and he stood aside as the tiger entered. I wanted to pass out; my knees were weak.

Smiley reentered the code.

The gate shut, the *bang* echoing in my mind.

"Get back, get back!" Brad shouted at us.

* * *

At the building door, Smiley lifted his arm, turned his head away, and dropped his arm. He entered the building and slammed the door shut.

The tiger launched itself straight for Brad. It was impressive, the speed, the brute force. I turned away. My senses heightened; Brad's screams reverberated in my head as I cowered with Aleem in the enclosure's corner.

Beneath the rubble of the wall that had fallen in my mind, something dormant awoke. The nausea of the guilt and the crippling fear had become an explosive cocktail. I'd passed through a primal barrier in my mind.

Fuck this.

I ripped off my coat and my light-blue shirt—the last piece of my humanity—and there I stood barechested in the cold night. I grabbed the branch Brad had used on the fox.

Aleem stayed in the corner of the enclosure. "Please, someone help us," he screamed as his face contorted to resemble a deranged killer in a low-budget horror film. He wasn't praying anymore. Any help would suffice.

Brad's mangled body lay lifeless a few steps ahead of me. I raised the branch above my head.

Let's see how tough you are if I stick this in your brain.

The raw hunger to kill pumped throughout my veins, fueling me. I lost myself.

"Arrgghhh!" I shouted, staring the beast down.

He didn't flinch, but instead he rocked back onto his steel legs, standing tall.

I saw crude serrated blades around his body and meshes of barbed wire above his paws, which had long sharpened claws. A hydraulic sound choked the air around me, the blades around his body moving up and down. This hack-job of a beast suggested they were far from perfection. His purpose, however, was clear...to kill.

I aimed the sharp end of the branch at the tiger's left eye, but he dodged. Leaping to the side, I faced him. His steel paw crashed into my cheek. My body toppled over. The force was magnificent yet brutal, and I landed on my stomach, unable to move. My face was on fire, ripped open by the tiger's razor-sharp claws.

An awkward pressure pushed on my back. As I looked at my limp, outstretched arm, my wristwatch shone under the artificial zoo lights. Its ticking thundered in my mind. *Tick... Tick... Tick.*

Clarity reigned.

Our earth, which for centuries we'd maltreated, had decided to change course. And now we'd given its other inhabitants, who we'd slaughtered and shunned, a way to fight back. The animal cyborgs had risen. And like the ticking in my mind, a countdown had commenced once we'd reached the apex of the species pyramid. A countdown to extinction, our own.

Nature, it seems, will find a way to protect herself, even if she must cheat.

THE SMALL HOURS BROADCAST

"Did you hear that?" Carmen raised herself up against the headboard. The maroon comforter crept down to her waist.

She received no reply.

Each passing second in the pitch-black room caused her breath to quicken. She scanned the bedroom, seeking any trace of light to verify her surroundings. After a few swings of her head, she discovered the alarm clock's digits and their glow. Concentrating on the shapes around the clock, she made out a few items: a framed photo of her and her husband, her hair dryer, and a vase that held no flowers.

She whispered, "Hey, honey. Wake up. I heard something."

Again, she received no reply. She shook Michael's left shoulder, keeping on until a familiar groan broke the silence.

Michael said, "What? It's late, babe."

"I heard a noise, sounded like someone...well, it sounded like someone tapping something in the living room, I think."

Michael took too long to reply, and Carmen shook his shoulder again.

"Stop shaking me. I am trying to listen. Good grief, did you see the time?"

Carmen hadn't registered the time. She focused on the alarm clock, which revealed it was thirty-six minutes past one. She shook her head.

Who cares what time it is?

She said, "For the third time, do you hear anything?"

"Yeah, yeah, the dripping, it's just the shower. You know it does that sometimes. I must have forgotten to close it properly. No reason to get bent out of shape over it."

"No, it's not that, Michael. I heard a different tapping sound and it didn't come from the bathroom."

"Okay, okay, I'm listening again."

As she waited, Carmen clenched her fingers into tight-balled fists, hoping he would hear the foreign sound when it returned and take care of the problem—no matter how silly it turned out to be.

The tapping sound returned. It was as clear as any sound Carmen had heard in her existence.

"There, there," she whispered.

"Carmen, I don't hear anything."

I can't believe he's being such a dick.

Her shoulders tensed as if two claws had grasped down on them. She fought against a wave of tears that wanted to break out and inhaled deep, then exhaled slowly. When able to speak, she said, "Aren't you going to take a look? What kind of man are you? What if it's a burglar?"

"Oh please, Carmen. I hear nothing, and you know I have to be up early tomorrow morn—"

Carmen squeezed his shoulder, this time with all her might, hoping all the inner turmoil rising within her would flood through him.

"Stop that," he said. "I'm going to sleep. You are overtired, but feel free to walk around the house in the middle of the night, like a fool, for nothing."

"You can be a real asshole when you want, you know that?"

Michael didn't reply.

She turned on her bedside light, immediately comforted by the warm yellow glow illuminating her surroundings. A brief thought of grabbing her pillow to launch an assault on Michael passed.

Carmen listened. The tapping had ceased, but she remained unnerved.

I'll close the shower properly, in case the sound comes back, and then he'll have to admit that he can hear it.

This plan of immediate action released some inner tension as she put any thoughts of inspecting the ominous tapping sound that came down the passage on hold. It helped that the bathroom was on the opposite side of the room to the passage.

She climbed out of bed, slipped her feet into her faded pink slippers, and journeyed the few yet labored steps to the bathroom. As she reached into the darkness, the hair on her outstretched arm stood up. She felt for the light switch against the bathroom's white tiled wall. The seconds ticked away in her mind like doors slamming shut.

Carmen tried to flick the light switch on, but failed to connect cleanly and thus failed to apply the required force.

Damn it.

She moved her hand back to the switch. This time she focused and felt the switch beneath her fingers.

She pressed down.

* * *

White light flooded the bathroom. Carmen shifted her gaze around the barren white tiled walls—barring a large mirror and medicine cabinet—with rapid, quick-fire movements. She glanced over at the shower, toilet, and bathroom countertop, the last of which was covered by an assortment of products. Her brain processed the expected and welcome images of her surroundings. She entered the bathroom with a step of confidence and walked a straight line to the shower.

Carmen opened the shower's glass door and placed one foot inside. She shook her head as she watched a drop of water form on the showerhead. Gravity pulled the drop into a free fall until it hit the powder-blue tiled shower floor—nearly hitting her pink slipper. She turned the shower handle, closing it tight. Another drop of water hit her hand, the frigid drop heightening her senses, and a chill retreated down her spine. She sensed something behind her, and an urge to turn around enveloped her.

You're being silly. There's nothing.

She tapped her foot on the shower's floor as she waited to confirm the dripping had ceased. No more drops formed. Nodding to herself, she turned around, forcing herself to turn with the same speed as normal.

Nothing appeared behind her.

Halfway through the bathroom, she stopped mid-step. Something had set off another warning within her mind.

She put her foot down and turned to face the large mirror above the bathroom counter. There was an unexplainable feeling of irregularity in the reflected image. She focused and tried to figure out what seemed off.

Nothing presented itself, and instead, Carmen noticed her ruffled dark-brown shoulder-length hair and then her emerald-green eyes—which looked tired.

Maybe I do need some rest. Maybe Michael was right, and I am overtired and thus mistaken about the tapping I heard. The mind can play tricks on you when you're really tired.

A weight lifted from her shoulders, and procedural thoughts now surfaced. She frowned at her appearance, her skin paler than she could recall, and then there was the frumpy white T-shirt and the black sweatpants she wore. The new issues of disappointment began to replace the fears from earlier, a trade she was more than happy to make.

She stepped closer to the mirror, even managing to

smile at the idea of wearing something provocative tomorrow night to surprise Michael. The thoughts of what would ensue if she did helped break the remaining shackles of the earlier fears. Feeling the best she had all night, she ran the cold tap in the washbasin below the mirror, splashed some of its cool water over her face, and looked up.

The words *Help me* were scrawled over the center of the mirror, as if someone had blown their breath and written with their finger. Carmen's eyes widened. She blinked. The words remained. The chill returned, enveloping her rib cage, and her heart pounded inside her chest with renewed vigor.

Clarity hit.

Michael, you bastard.

She was about to turn and go curse her husband for playing such childish tricks on her, when a black cloak-like shadow flapped behind her. It was brief but awoke primal instincts—fight or flight. The feeling of someone behind her resurfaced, and she looked to the right of her reflection in the mirror.

"Michael! Michael! Help me!" Carmen screamed.

The flickering image of a pale-skinned, curly-haired blonde woman, dressed in a white bathrobe and reaching out with her hand, shook Carmen to the core. It took a split second for the adrenaline to course through her veins.

Run.

Before another thought had time to form, she'd darted out of the bathroom.

She fell over the bed in her haste to reach Michael, who bolted straight up, his widened eyes locked onto his wife.

"What? What is it?" He switched on his bedside light, which brought much-needed illumination.

"There is someone...in the bathroom," Carmen said. Her face drained of warmth as her body shook.

"The bedroom's bathroom?"

"Yes."

Michael nodded. Carmen felt a sense of hope cradle her, knowing the expression on his face to be serious.

"Stay here," he said.

She nodded and gripped the comforter tight.

Michael walked toward the bathroom.

The next moment he was inside.

* * *

Carmen's heart thundered within her chest, reverberating in her head.

The seconds ticked on in her mind. She braced through a shudder as she awaited Michael's reassurance. She couldn't handle the suspense.

She said, "Michael. Are you there?"

"I don't see anything," Michael replied from within the bathroom.

"What?"

"There is no one here."

Carmen released her grip on the comforter and moved off the bed. She stood and walked toward the bathroom.

Michael passed her as she was about to enter the

bathroom. "Please, Carmen. I need to get some sleep."

She didn't reply. The doorway leading into the bathroom stole her attention. She bit her bottom lip, realizing she needed to cross the threshold again. Steadying herself, she blocked out the haunting image of her last trip to the bathroom.

She entered.

There is no stranger.

She walked toward the mirror.

There is no writing.

Her reflection was all she saw. She pushed through her frayed nerves and waited for something to happen, but nothing did. After a minute or two, her body found some sense of its usual equilibrium.

No woman, nothing is out of the ordinary. I must have imagined it. Yeah, that's it. It was such a quick glimpse, and I've heard of people who imagine things when overtired. Yeah, it's definitely a symptom from lack of sleep. Now that I think about it, I can barely even recall how she looked.

Carmen left the bathroom and took a seat on her side of the bed. Michael was asleep, facing the opposite wall. She reached toward the switch for her bedside light and paused, holding the comfort the light brought. After telling herself this wasn't the behavior of a grown woman, she gripped the switch.

Tap...tap...tap, tap, tap.

Her body froze, as if it had plunged into Arctic waters.

No, not the tapping again.

She contemplated waking Michael, but his earlier cold demeanor stopped her.

Fuck this. I will check what's going on.

Having endured enough of the cat-and-mouse game with her fears, she willed herself calm and once more relegated the thoughts of impending doom to the back of her overtired mind.

I will go check, and it will be something stupid. Then I can finally sleep.

* * *

Carmen made her way to the passageway, regretting not taking up the electrician's offer of installing lights in the passageway when they had first bought the home. Instead, they had opted for the bare minimum when it came to repairs and new installations. That was over three months ago. The parsimoniousness had led her to the current predicament of requiring the dim glow her cell phone provided to traverse the darkness of the narrow passageway.

Having exited the bedroom, Carmen wouldn't have to wait long to escape the dark. A faint light was flickering ahead of her against the wall on her left. Her pace toward the illuminated area, slow at first, quickened as she realized what it was.

She entered the living room, from where the light source came, shaking her head. She didn't even bother to switch on the room's light.

Damn it, Michael. You left the television on again.

She sighed. A wave of relief washed over her as she realized the TV had been the source of the strange noises. The woman she had seen in the bathroom must have been nothing more than the effects of an overtired mind.

Carmen smiled, wanting to laugh at herself.

She walked over to the coffee table, picked up the remote, and turned to face the TV. Some or other war documentary in black and white filled the screen. She changed the channel, an instinctive reflex.

"So you believe we have to reach a different state of awareness to receive these thoughts?" the blonde woman on the screen, wearing a charcoal power suit, asked.

"Yes," the old gray-haired man in a neat navy-blue suit answered. "I believe when our senses are heightened, especially in extreme circumstances, we send out these waves. For the receiver to be able to intercept, interpret, and process them, they must be in a different state than our regular consciousness. I believe the key aspects to be: the heightened state of the sender and the altered state of the receiver, for this to work."

The man coughed. "Excuse me... These aspects are either pushing the limits of normal conscious thought or not being shackled by it. For instance, I have studied some people who, while dreaming in bed or even sleepwalking, later claimed to be witnessing events unrelated to them. I've even looked into people having déjà vu when meeting a person for the first time. These events are all possible cases."

A caption with his name appeared on the bottom of

the screen. It read *Professor Heinrich Stein-Wolff*.

Professor Stein-Wolff continued, "Imagine one is in a great state of either ecstasy or fear and then broadcasts these thoughts to the universe as brain waves. Some liken it to a form of telepathy, the transference of these images, sounds or smells and even—"

Carmen pressed the *off* switch.

What a load of shit. This is the nonsense people who should be asleep end up watching.

Covered in darkness, she used the light from the cell phone to guide her back to the room. She shook her head as she thought about the night's adventure.

How silly I have been.

She entered the passageway. Her warm and comfy bed called her.

Tap...tap...tap, tap, tap.

Carmen gasped, and a grunt-like sound escaped from her throat as the extra air came rushing in. Her arm jolted as she shined the light from the cell phone toward the noise. A noise she knew was coming from right in front of her.

At first her brain refused to believe the information it received from her eyes, but as she held her gaze, the horror remained.

There was a balding man, dressed in a tailored suit and hanging with a rope around his neck, right in the center of the passageway, barely two steps from her. His polished brown work shoes dangled above the floor, and she watched as the right foot reached toward the floor.

Tap...tap...tap, tap, tap.

The sound of the right shoe tapping on the floor echoed in her head. She looked up, but the man's eyes were shut and his pallid face expressionless. As fast as the right foot had moved, it returned to hanging in the air, in unison with the left.

"Mi...Mi...Michael." Carmen could barely talk, her words merely a whisper. Her body froze, from the extremities in, as the shock took control. Her legs weakened, and she had to lean against the wall of the passageway to keep her balance. She fought back. Adrenaline pumped and with it her strength returned.

She bolted for the bedroom, screaming.

* * *

"Carmen, wake up," the voice said. She felt someone shaking her shoulder. The voice repeated, "Carmen, wake up."

She realized it was Michael, and he was still shaking her as she opened her eyes, her body drenched in sweat. "What? What happened?" she asked.

"You were having a nightmare. You scared the shit out of me." Michael rubbed her shoulder.

Carmen looked around the room. All the lights were on.

The time on the alarm clock read 2:17 a.m.

"Man, that must have been some nightmare. You screamed like crazy," Michael said, concern etched into his face.

"Yeah, it was." She couldn't believe how real it had all felt.

The sounds of sirens neared.

The sirens' whines continued to rise in volume. Michael made his way to the window and peered out. Carmen didn't move.

"Wonder what's happening?" he asked. "Oh, there goes an ambulance and a police vehicle...and another police car. Come check this out."

"No."

Michael shrugged. "I'm going to check the local news for anything on all those cops."

Carmen could see the intrigue in Michael's face. She didn't reply. Instead, she pulled the comforter over her chest and buried her head into her pillow. She heard Michael exit the bedroom.

She couldn't get back to sleep, fragmented images of the nightmare flashing over and over in her mind's eye. After nearly half an hour, she heard footsteps approaching, and she raised her head slightly, watching the doorway.

Michael stuck his head in. "Hey, you should see this. It's all over the local news."

"What?"

"Some guy, not even two blocks from us, on Straub Street, strangled his wife in their bathroom. Neighbors heard her screams and phoned the cops, but they were too late and found him hanging in the passageway. They say he was already dressed for work. Isn't that the oddest thing?" Michael said, shaking his head.

Carmen didn't respond.

Michael sighed. "Well, that's what they're

speculating on the news."

Again, she kept still.

Michael took a seat on the bed alongside her and stroked her shoulder again. "I'm sorry, babe. Forget all the other shit. What was your nightmare about? Do you remember?"

Carmen couldn't look at him. Her body felt void of energy and once more the grip of an ominous frigid chill held her. Horrifying images of her nightmare kept invading her thoughts. She tried to fight back.

It was a bad dream, just a coincidence what Michael saw on the news.

"Well? You remember it?" Michael asked.

She turned over, facing away from him. "I don't remember it."

"Come on now, babe."

"I said I don't remember. Now leave me alone." She shut her eyes.

Just a bad dream, just a coincidence.

Carmen clutched the comforter tightly around herself.

NESSIE LIVES

Nightfall had found the bank by the river. Carlton Thompson proceeded with on-scene patchwork to a plastic dinosaur head. His best friend, Reed, was seated on a large broken branch talking to another of their friends, Aimee. Around them towering trees stood proud, while birds chirped. The spicy, earthy aroma of bushes and plants tickled his sense of smell.

The river was well known, but they knew of a remote area perfect for their plan. Today, the perfect night for their operation had arrived: Halloween. While the town was preoccupied with trick-or-treating, they set up an event, hoping it would become a story enshrined in local legend.

Carlton, noticing darkness had fallen over him, lifted his head. His gaze was drawn to the surface of the river. Certain spots glimmered, almost as if there were crystals reflecting the moon's light beneath the water's surface.

Carlton said, "Hey, Reed. You're meant to be giving me a hand."

Reed looked up and frowned. "I did. I'm the one who found the old head, after all."

"Yeah? And who fixed it to look more like a sea monster?"

"You did, but who mentioned this spot?"

"Yeah, yeah. Listen, I've attached the head to the plastic base. It should float, but we've got to get a move on. It's already night and we need to take some shots."

"Well, let's do this, then." Reed reached into his pocket for his smartphone.

Carlton nodded.

Aimee looked uninterested. She wasn't a fan of nature and preferred the hustle and bustle of town. Yet, she had asked to come along, as usual, and Carlton already recognized the sulk that deepened in her visage. Soon, they would have to listen to her complaints all the way home.

Carlton put her mood out of the forefront of his mind.

They had important work to do.

The river had been subject to strange legends before. None stuck. From a dreadlocked monster that sat in the trees, to a Bigfoot-type creature that roamed the shores, to spirits that lived beneath the surface. This time, however, Carlton and Reed, two veteran pranksters, believed they had the know-how for a decent crack at creating one that would live on. Sure, copying a Loch Ness Monster-type creature wasn't very original, but it had an allure and style that the older people of town would fall for. With the added romance of Halloween, the plan appeared foolproof.

Carlton, wearing cargo shorts, waded into the water with the plesiosaur-looking cryptid head on its base. They had decided to name their creation Nessie 2.0. He pushed it into the river. The current was weak, which he was glad about.

"Right. Take some shots. We can edit them later for the best," Carlton said, making his way back to land.

Reed started taking photos. Nessie 2.0 seemed to stand stationary on the water, giving them time to take photos from different angles and distances. After a few minutes, Carlton tapped Reed's shoulder.

"You done? I want to get it out before the current picks up and takes it away. It won't help our legend if someone finds it."

"Just a few more."

Aimee let out a grunt. "Guys, let's get going. It's cold and dark, and I need to pee."

"Almost done," Carlton said, realizing it would indeed be a long journey home.

"You guys and your damn silly ideas. Don't know why I said I would come along. No one is going to fall for this."

Reed shook his head. "Damn it, Aimee. Go pee in the bushes if it's such an emergency and quit whining."

A splash of water exploded mere inches from Nessie 2.0. Both Reed and Carlton turned to look at Aimee, who was picking up stones around her. Her cheeks flared red, and Carlton knew there would be no reasoning with her.

"Aimee. Don't be stupid," Reed said.

"Aimee. We're almost done." Carlton held up his hand. "Think how funny this will be when it makes the front page of the local paper. Just imagine the headline *Nessie Lives*, and hey, you never know, maybe it will make a few other papers. Oh, and think of all the conspiracy sites that will want a piece of it."

"No," Reed said. "Stop sympathizing with her. She chose to come along. If she wants to throw a tantrum, she should leave."

"That's not—"

"I'm out." Aimee tossed the bunch of rocks in her hand toward them. She cursed them both beneath her breath as she left them in her wake, disappearing into the wall of trees that surrounded the river.

"Women, huh," Reed said.

"It's not necessary to be so hard on her." Carlton shrugged. "Anyway, I'm going to bring Nessie Two in."

"Just a couple more."

Before Carlton could reply, a harsh rustling sound came toward them from the trees. The loudness suggested something large headed their way, not a little critter. Carlton held his breath, then exhaled when Aimee reappeared. He wanted to scold her for frightening him, but stopped when noticing her face was drained of color and her clothes were dirty as if she had taken a few tumbles in the dirt.

"You okay?" Carlton asked.

"Holy shit," Aimee said. "There are these things, like people, but they're gray. They're everywhere. Guys, something isn't right. I'm scared. We have to get out of here, but we can't go that way."

"Funny," Reed said, "but we aren't falling for that shit."

Something about her shaking hands and strained eyes didn't suggest a prank. Carlton approached her, but she turned away and ran. Where was she going? He watched her intersect him and Reed.

Fully clothed, Aimee dived into the river.

* * *

It was as if Carlton had left his body and was looking down on himself. The view he imagined of his inert self resembled stuffed animals he had seen in museums. Reed, however, jolted into action, running toward the water.

"Aimee. What the hell are you doing?"

Aimee didn't reply. She seemed hell-bent on making it across.

Carlton managed to will reanimation upon himself; slowly, he turned around. He studied the trees, trying to understand what could have startled Aimee. The idea of it being a poor joke was long gone. He considered it being some type of wild animal, as that was possible all the way out here. Images of bears, wolves, and snakes came to the fore of his mind, but she had said people, *gray people*.

Reed walked into his line of sight. "She's gone mad. She's really going to swim across the river. What do you think has gotten into her?"

A shadowy figure passed between the trees behind Reed. Another figure shifted to the right. The blurry forms stopped moving and evolved into shapes he could recognize. He understood why Aimee had called them gray people, but as his gaze remained transfixed on them, he realized they looked more like something else: *ghosts*. Unable to speak, he managed to raise his arm and point.

Reed, frowning, turned around. "What the hell is it?"

Carlton mumbled, "I-I think we have to run."

He didn't wait for Reed to agree; instead, he bolted toward the river. Reed's heavy steps trailed right behind him—at least he hoped they were Reed's. He looked for Aimee before jumping into the water. She had almost reached the other side. A sudden change in the weather took control, and even though his body heated up from the exertion, it wasn't enough to blanket against the new frigid chill in the atmosphere.

Carlton splashed through the water. When he was deep enough to swim, he launched his body forward.

In the middle of the river, he lifted his head and caught sight of Aimee on land. She hurried back toward him, waving her hands above her head. Carlton, who wasn't as athletic as Aimee or Reed, felt his arms yearn for a rest, but the look on Aimee's face told him there would be no respite. His heart beat so strong he could feel it in his throat, and he stopped his splashing, attempting to float, hoping to hear what she said.

"They're coming from this side too. We have to swim. We have to keep swimming downriver," Aimee shouted.

She ran and dived back in.

* * *

Aimee headed downriver.

"Get moving," Reed said, passing Carlton. "We need to follow her."

Carlton, floating in the middle of the river, watched Reed swimming after Aimee. He didn't follow. His lungs burned and something ominous within him told him there was no escape. He thought about the failed urban legends attached to the river, praying for a way out of the mess he found himself in. One legend, where the spirits of the dead were believed to live in a part of the river, kept hammering at a door in his mind. He opened the door, hit the light switch, and searched the room wherein the legend resided, trying to remember what he could about the tale. Only bits of info appeared. One thing he recalled was that spirits could only leave the river at certain times, except these things were all coming back. Were they returning under the shroud of night to wait until they could leave again? Did they have more freedom on Halloween to move about as they pleased? If that was the case, he and his friends had picked the worst possible day to come to the river.

They were trapped.

He took short, quick breaths.

The gray people as Aimee called them, or ghosts as Carlton now truly believed them to be, kept approaching. When they paused before the water, Carlton found himself begging internally that they would halt their progress and turn away. The darkness of night only compounded the dread that held him, and he found himself with no plan of action.

One of the ghosts reached into the water with its arm. The water remained unmoved. When the ghost lifted its limb out of the water and held the appendage up, Carlton saw an aged pale hand and arm, different from the featureless gray blur of the rest of the figure. It seemed as if the water gave them some sustenance of life. The ghost took a step into the water; the ghosts on either side of the river followed its lead.

Carlton's chest contracted.

They were all getting in.

He had forgotten about Reed and Aimee trying to escape—though he thought he might've heard intermittent screaming ahead—as his brain still fought to find some rational explanation for his current predicament. None arose. The ghosts, however, kept coming. Carlton watched with mouth agape as they seemed to float with only their feet in the water. The longer they were in the water, the less they looked like gray shapes. They all lightened and cleared. Carlton could see people, pale, translucent people that shimmered every time he blinked.

The legend of the spirits in the river was true.

Closer and closer they came.

All this would have intrigued Carlton had he not been fearful for his life. Yet, with the ghosts on him, no attack commenced. Instead, they sank, disappearing beneath the surface. It had taken only a moment and they were gone. Had he truly seen them? His mind informed him that he had. The fear that coursed through his veins confirmed it.

The urge to look beneath the surface was potent, but he forced himself not to. If he couldn't see them, maybe they were no longer there. He remembered Reed and Aimee, and he searched for them, but saw no one. There was no way they could have swum fast enough to escape his view. The icy thought that the ghosts had taken his friends below the surface of the water sent chills all over his body. Why had the ghosts taken his friends and left him? His body pumped adrenaline.

He needed to get to the shore.

He needed to get help.

Carlton was about to swim when a cold hand clutched onto his ankle. He attempted to kick it off, but the grip was too strong. Would anyone know what had happened here on this fateful Halloween night? How their attempt to create their own legend had seen them uncover one that was true, one that was dark, and from which there was no escape. How had the ghosts of the river managed to go almost undetected for so long?

Carlton cursed his bad luck.

Tears swelled in his eyes.

He gave one final attempt to swim away, only to feel another hand grip his other leg.

More hands wrapped around his legs.

Carlton was being pulled under.

He saw the moon, high in the nighttime Halloween sky, as he went below. Focusing, he kept staring at the moon, which became blurry from the water. A shape moved overhead, and for a second Carlton felt the warmth of hope burn in his chest, but it was immediately extinguished, along with it any thoughts of rescue.

The shape was only Nessie 2.0 floating by.